COSMIC MATE

STARGAZER ALIEN SPACE CRUISE BRIDES #2

TASHA BLACK

13TH STORY PRESS

13th Story Press

PO Box 506

Swarthmore, PA 19081

13thStoryPress@gmail.com

TASHA BLACK STARTER LIBRARY

COSMIC MATE

1

SERENA

S erena Scott resisted the urge to smooth her bun and adjust her glasses for the camera.

As it happened, her hair was down, her glasses were tucked away in her travel bag, and there were no cameras anywhere in sight.

She only wore the glasses for show anyway. Her PR people told her they played down her youthful features and made her look smarter to voters.

But tonight, she actually wanted to look her age, and maybe even act her age, for once.

Tonight, she had nothing to lose.

"Pretty lady," someone yelled over the music.

She turned to find a tall Bergalian smiling at her rakishly and holding out a furry paw.

"Want to dance?" His voice was deep but smooth.

Her mind instinctively played out the optics of being seen dancing with a Bergalian. They were in favor of sentient rights, but their views on space pollution were problematic at best.

"Yes," she said quickly, reminding herself that she was

here as a person, not as an ambassador. No one here on Bissmeee would care who she danced with, or even know who she was.

Frankly, she was doing her best to forget who she was herself for one night.

The Bergalian gently took her hand and led her into the press of bodies on the dance floor. Serena smiled up at him and he grinned back.

Then he began flinging his body heedlessly around in a way that seemed about as related to dancing as scribbling might be related to painting watercolors.

Serena watched him for a moment in total disbelief, and then he tugged at her hand, pulling her into a spin.

He smiled widely as she spun helplessly in to his side and then out again like a character in an antique cell-film.

He managed to step on her foot before spinning her out a second time, causing her to go slightly off balance and bump into a Cameliunak lady in a fancy dress.

"Excuse me," the woman trumpeted indignantly.

"I'm so sorry, ma'am," Serena said as she flew past.

A deep chuckle came from the shadows, but she couldn't locate who it belonged to. The Bergalian had pulled her close enough that his fur blocked most of her vision. He was wearing some kind of scented oil that was actually quite nice.

"Pretty lady," he said again, leering down at her.

Her instinct was to pull back.

But Serena Scott's instinct was always to pull back. She had spent a lifetime trying not to offend, not to make a mistake, not to be too loud or too aggressive, or too timid or too boring.

I got left at the altar.

All my constituents hate me.

Tonight, I'm going to do something excessive.

That had been her plan, at least. But she wasn't actually sure she wanted that excessive something to be crash-dancing with a half-drunk Bergalian.

"Excuse me, sir, may I cut in?" It was the deep voice again, matching the laugh from the shadows.

The Bergalian was so surprised that he froze in place.

His sudden stillness almost sent Serena toppling.

Before she had a chance, she felt strong hands on her shoulders, steadying her.

"Be my guest," the Bergalian said in a friendly way. "Come find me to dance again later, if you want," he whispered to Serena.

She smiled at him, not really sure what to say.

He waved a gigantic arm in a furry arc and disappeared into the crowd.

Serena turned to see who held her.

Large brown eyes gazed down at her steadily from a face so chiseled it could have belonged to a statue. A pair of wickedly curved horns extended backward from his forehead.

An equally sculpted body was just barely hidden by a tight white t-shirt over low-slung leather breeches.

A familiar tattoo showed on his right forearm.

"A Maltaffian bodyguard," she heard herself murmur too low for him to hear.

"Yeah, but I'm off-duty tonight," he replied with a teasing half-smile.

Antitha's Belt, he's got shifter-level hearing.

"I'm so sorry," she said, mortified. "I guess it's been too long since I was off-planet."

"Don't worry about it," he replied. "Can I get you a drink or are you committed to dying on the dance floor?"

"Gods no," she replied. "When he asked me to dance, I didn't quite realize what he had in mind."

"But you didn't try to stop him," the Maltaffian said.

"I'm trying to be open-minded," she replied, feeling stupid as soon as the words were out of her mouth.

But the Maltaffian just nodded. "I'm Ozmarck, but you can call me Oz."

"Nice to meet you," she said. "I'm Serena. You can call me... Serena."

She had forgotten to lie about her name.

But if he recognized her, he gave no indication. He merely nodded and offered her his arm.

They traveled to the bar together through a crowd of dancers from all over the galaxy. Serena had never seen so many races together at once without weapons or protest signs.

Frankly, it was giving her hope for her own troubled system.

"Sampler at my usual table," Oz yelled to the bartender.

The humanoid inclined his head.

Oz led Serena further from the fray.

When they reached the curve of the outer wall, she realized there were cushions and floating tables in a series of shadowy recesses.

"After you," Oz said, gesturing toward a small table with golden cushions.

Serena slid behind the table and lowered herself to one of the cushions.

"I didn't even see these tables before," she said.

"I enjoy my privacy," Oz replied, stretching out on the cushion beside hers. "Besides, this is a great spot for people-watching."

The table lowered itself to a perfect height for them, and Serena felt instantly cozy.

The big Maltaffian was right, the people-watching was incredible from this vantage point.

Her furry former dance partner had found himself a new match. The woman had a silvery veil covering what appeared to be a head covered in delicate tentacles. Her six tapered legs gave her a decided advantage at staying right-side up as the Bergalian flung her around the dance floor. After a particularly violent spin, she tilted her head back and laughed as the Bergalian gazed down at her in a decidedly love-struck way.

"You see, you were just four legs shy of being able to keep up with him," Oz teased.

"They look amazing," Serena said, shaking her head in disbelief.

"That's what I like about this place," Oz said.

"What?" she asked.

"Neutral ground," he said simply. "As long as the Cerulean soldiers stay out, this place will be an intergalactic paradise."

Serena bit her lip. This was supposed to be a break from politics. But Cerulean soldiers were half the reason she was going on her honeymoon alone.

She needed a break from the threats and fury on her home planet after she had supported legislation that essentially backed up everything Oz had just said.

Cerulean soldiers had no reason to occupy her sector. The bands of soldiers sowed fear and resentment wherever they went.

She had voted to limit Cerulean interference to cases where the soldiers were summoned or emergency forces were needed in general.

Her holo-box had exploded immediately with messages from outraged citizens. She suspected most of them were members of the gentry who viewed Cerulean occupation as protective of their interests.

Messages from the Cerulean labor unions had been less emotional, but more vaguely threatening.

Her security back home had been more than happy to have her trip off-planet continue as scheduled, even when her fiancé decided he'd rather head for the hills than marry a controversial public figure.

Now here she was, a woman of a certain age, her last likely prospect for marriage and children gone with the wind.

But somehow she felt quite happy, curled up on a cushion beside the horned guard, watching the universe dance past.

She glanced over at him and almost did a double-take.

He had been gazing at her thoughtfully, but when their eyes met the air between them seemed to electrify.

2

OZMARCK

Ozmarck gazed, dumbfounded, at the fragile human as lightning coursed through his veins.

Emotion tore at him, threatening to suck his mind into a black hole of need.

I just met her...

But it didn't matter. Suddenly, nothing mattered.

A lead weight of desire dropped on him, heavy as an anchor.

And he knew the feeling for exactly what it was.

He had found his true mate. Now his body was launching into the mating thrall, leaving him no time to wonder at the sudden change in his life and priorities.

The bartender approached, carrying a tray of food and beverages so heavy he nearly staggered under it.

"Come with me," Oz managed to growl to. Serena through a clenched jaw.

"But, sir, your food," the bartender said.

"Bring it to my rooms, leave it at the door," Oz snapped.

The woman was slowly lifting herself from her cushion, as if in a dream.

She probably had no idea - about the true bond or the thrall.

He nearly pitied her, but the demands of his body allowed him no room for conversation.

He offered her his hand and she took it.

They set off through the press of the crowd, but her pace was too slow. And there were too many other males, scenting her, leering at her.

His protective instinct amped up and he swept her into his arms.

"Wh-what's happening?"

Her whispered words seared into his ravenous flesh, soft breath awakening each nerve ending.

He clutched her closer and broke into a sprint.

"What do you know about Maltaffian bonds and the rites of the thrall?" he asked her, the words tearing out of him as if they preferred to stay in and let his body do the talking.

"I'm just trying to take a night off," she murmured into his chest. "Have some fun for once..."

By the red rings of Cylonius, she has no idea.

Well, if she was looking for some fun, she was about to find it.

He reached his room and slammed his palm against the sensor. After an eternity, the door slid open to reveal a monastic space.

Oz traveled cheap when he was on his own dime. There was just room for a large bed, a small chair, a case and a door to the bath.

It didn't matter. They would only need the bed.

And as soon as he got his mouth on her she would forget her surroundings anyway.

A surge of lust nearly turned him inside out, and he tossed her to the bed as the door slid closed behind them.

"Ohhh," she moaned, arms out to him.

He smiled.

She felt it too, the bond that stretched tight, nearly choking him the moment she was out of his arms.

He crawled in after her, stripping his t-shirt over his head.

She grabbed his upper arms, her soft fingers tightening over hard muscle.

"You're mine," he growled.

But she was too busy fumbling with the tie on his breeches to take any notice of his words.

Words were meaningless now. They were both in the thrall.

She was a proper female, conscious of manners and niceties, he could tell by her gracious handling of the Bergalian earlier and by the quality of the clothing Oz was ripping off her right now.

Any other night she would have died before tearing at his pants frantically with her fingernails.

He swiped her hands off him and took off his leathers himself, flinging them against the wall where they nearly bounced back onto the bed in the tiny space.

When he turned back, she was pawing at her own silken undergarments.

"Easy, baby," he groaned, battling his own panic to shred her bra and panties.

Her skin was warm and feverish to the touch. She was deeply in the thrall now.

He forced himself to take a breath and speak to her. It was wrong for her not to know what was happening.

"I will always protect you," he told her. "I will treasure you always."

But before he could voice the vows he intended, or explain what was happening, she went up on her elbows to press her lips to his.

He saw stars behind his eyelids, universes expanding and collapsing, the passage of time and space.

She moaned against his mouth.

He pressed her to the bed, pinning her warm, soft body with his hardness.

3

SERENA

Serena was lost in a sea of sensation.

Oz owned her senses, his delicious scent hypnotizing her as she struggled to absorb the ecstasy of his enormous body against hers, the heat, the pulse of his huge and rigid cock against her hip, the sound of his raspy voice, the taste of his possessive kiss.

She closed her eyes, and when she opened them again, he was kissing down her collarbone, flicking his tongue against a nipple.

His tongue seemed slightly longer than a human's, strong and hot, and certainly more clever.

Her blood sang with lust.

Serena had never experienced anything like this. She reached for him, needing to touch some part of him.

Her fingers slid across the smooth, ridged surface of his left horn.

He moaned as if in pain, but leaned into her hand.

A pang of desire had her almost doubled-over with the frantic need to feel him inside her.

He seemed to sense this, but he only moved lower, licking a hot trail down her belly, across her hip.

Serena froze with anticipation as he nudged her legs apart.

When his incredible tongue lashed against her sex, she almost blacked out with the pleasure.

"Ohh, Serena," he moaned against her.

She could feel a tide rising inside, like stillness before the storm on an open sea.

"Please," she whimpered, hands out to him, needing them to be one, afraid the riptide would carry her away if he wasn't merged with her, holding her down.

He crawled up to cage her head in his muscular arms.

"Mine," he growled.

His eyes were hazy with lust and she saw her face reflected in them but almost didn't recognize herself, her expression was so desperate.

His hardness pressed against her for just a second before he thrust deeply into her.

There should have been pain, but she only felt soul-shuddering relief.

He stilled, but she sank her nails into his shoulders and lifted her hips, needing the next thrust more than she needed her next breath.

He roared and thrust into her again and again, filling her, sending her higher and higher.

At last Serena nearly lifted off the bed with the pleasure.

Oz bit down on her neck and she felt herself flying as he cried out his own ecstasy, jetting into her again and again, extending her pleasure until she thought she could take no more.

When it was done, she was overcome with weariness.

The sudden need for sleep was almost scary, but the wild heat of his body wrapped around hers reassured Serena as the last moment of consciousness fled her exhausted system.

4

SERENA

S erena awoke feeling wildly happy.

She stretched and opened her eyes in the darkness, momentarily confused.

Where am I?

Why am I so warm?

Why am I so happy?

She sat up and felt strong arms around her, tugging her back down.

Oh, yeah.

She turned back.

Her horned lover was still asleep, though he clutched her to him, even in his slumber. In the soft light of the solar clock on his bedside table, she could see the ridges of muscle, the blue tone of the tattoo on his arm, and the serene, but somehow still possessive look on his handsome face.

Serena felt a wave of lust and had to fight back the urge to wake him up and beg him to take her again.

But that would not do. She couldn't miss her cruise.

And besides, now that her night of passion was over, she had to get serious.

Ambassador Serena Scott had just been dumped. She couldn't make a fool out of herself for a Maltaffian guard who was only looking for a one-night stand.

Even if that one-night stand was the most mind-blowing experience of her life...

But he was clutching her like she was the last escape pod key on a compromised ship.

How was she supposed to get out of here?

She looked around and spotted a body pillow beside her. She grabbed it and hugged it close, then rolled over.

When his arms sought her again, she deftly replaced herself with the pillow.

He moaned a little, but didn't wake up. She eased herself off the bed as quickly as she dared, and then dressed as best she could in the dim light.

Her underthings were in tatters. In the heat of the moment, she would have sworn she'd never need them again. Now that seemed like a bit of an oversight. She shoved them in the pocket of her dress, figuring she could go commando until she reached her storage locker at Bissmeee Port.

When she reached the door, she turned back for one last look.

Oz's broad back curled around the pillow he was holding, his muscular body juxtaposing with the sweetness of the way he cradled her replacement.

Her heart thumped with something like love, and she turned away, chiding herself for being such a baby.

Other women were able to fulfill their sexual desires without getting attached. Serena should be able to do the same.

She scurried out of the room, almost tripping over the food cart, and strode down the hallway, trying to remember how they'd gotten here so she could get back out again. After a few wrong turns, she made it out into the lobby of the club.

"Shuttle service to Bissmeee Port," a small robot called out helpfully.

She joined the weary-looking group of travelers that followed the glide-bot toward the exit.

She smiled when she saw the big furry Bergalian looking very sleepy, his arm tucked snugly around his six-legged companion from last night.

So she hadn't been the only one to have a little hook-up.

Though judging from the way the lady was smiling as she leaned her head against the Bergalian's chest, maybe theirs was more than a hook-up.

Serena felt a wave of loneliness and tamped it down hard.

She was a very lucky woman - lucky in her career, lucky in her friendships. You couldn't be lucky in everything, so it wasn't the end of the world to be unlucky in love.

The glass wall of the club slid open to reveal the flat dusty surface of Bissmeee.

A hover train stood waiting, the magnetized track field almost invisible under the swirling dirt.

"All aboard," the robotic conductor cried.

Serena clambered onto the last car, sitting in a rear-facing seat near the back so as to avoid conversation.

The car wobbled as the final passengers ascended. Once everyone was seated, it lurched forward, the standard recorded message about keeping appendages inside the carriage playing at a low level.

Serena watched the club disappear over the horizon as they sped away.

Maybe it was only that she hadn't eaten breakfast that morning - or dinner last night, come to think of it - but she felt suddenly hollowed out inside, empty like she might never be filled again.

5

OZMARCK

Oz paced the tiny room, his blood sizzling in his veins.

Where is she?

But it didn't matter.

Serena was gone. His heightened senses told him she had been gone since before Bissmeee's primary star was fully risen.

His comm unit dinged, bringing him out of his thoughts.

A message from the client.

He clenched his fists and tried to convince himself to breathe.

His last job had been a bust. Working for that two-bit excuse for a king was the worst career decision he'd ever made. Oz only hoped his reputation hadn't been too tarnished by the whole fiasco. He was really going to need the credits from this next gig if he was about to go on an intergalactic hunt for his mate.

He racked his brain for any clue as to where she might have been headed, but he couldn't remember her mentioning a single detail of her plans while they were in the club.

And then they had been too busy mating to speak anymore.

His body surged with lust at the thought of it, and he gasped, grabbing the headboard of the bed and nearly snapping it like a twig in his massive fist.

Find her. I have to find her...

But Bissmeee was a launch point to so many destinations. Without a clue, and without credits, it was impossible.

Serena...

He had a first name. No origin, no designation, no details. Except for her silky hair, her languid gaze, the rich hot pulse of her sex, the melody of her cries...

The headboard cracked in his hand, making a sound like gunshot.

His comm unit dinged again.

He grabbed his case and headed to the lobby. He had no choice but to hop the next shuttle and get to work. As soon as he had the credits, he would drop everything to chase her.

I will find you, Serena...

The hallway was crowded with weary travelers carrying their cases resolutely toward the glass exit doors.

"Shuttle service to Bissmeee Port," a robot called.

Oz followed it out to the hover train and boarded in the back, hoping he would have the seat to himself so he could think.

The train jolted forward, and he felt a wave of hopefulness.

He went over all he knew about his mate.

She was human, which narrowed things considerably as far as her origins.

She didn't live on Bissmeee - she had said she was off-planet.

She knew he was a Maltaffian guard. Most beings in the central rings would recognize the tattoo, but that did narrow out a few of the far-flung reaches.

And she had said more than once that she was trying to have fun, trying to enjoy a night off.

This meant that in spite of the quality of her garments, she was not in the upper classes. She worked at something, though he didn't know what.

And that was all he had - which was almost nothing, really.

The impossibility of finding her with so little information hit him like a sledge-craft and he closed his eyes against the hazy glow of the sun through the dust clouds.

But a little voice in the back of his head reminded him that until yesterday he had not located his mate yet at all.

Surely it would be easier to find her a second time than to happen upon her the first time. At least now he knew who he was looking for.

And he had claimed her.

His blood rushed through his ears at the thought, and he felt a rush of euphoria.

Now that he had claimed her, she would feel the draw to him as well. He wasn't just trying to find a needle in a haystack.

That needle would be trying to find him, too.

They were caught in each other's gravity, like a pair of binary stars.

Another jolt of pain struck him as he realized that if he'd had a bank full of credits, he could have stayed right where he was so that she could come back to him when she realized life had lost its meaning without him by her side.

He slid his communicator out of his pocket and stat-messaged his buddy, Ren, the bartender at the club.

OZMARCK:

If a woman with long dark hair comes looking for me, give her my comm code.

REN:

That's a first.

OZMARCK:

I mean it. If I give you a first name and a departure time, can you track someone?

THE FIRST RULE of hospitality on Bissmeee was discretion. But he had to ask.

REN:

You know I can't do that, buddy, sorry.

OZMARCK:

But if she comes, you'll give her my code?

REN:

Sure. Is something wrong? Did she take something from you?

. . .

SHE HAD TAKEN HIS HEART, his soul, his ability to live... She had taken his mate's bite.

OZMARCK:

Nope. I just need to tell her something.

REN:

Got it. I'll keep an eye out.

OZ SLID the device back in his pocket and tried to settle himself.

He was going to meet a big client, a dignitary of some kind. The pay-out on this job would be more than generous. They hadn't even released the name when they hired him, which always meant someone with deep pockets.

He'd complete the job first, then start the hunt for his mate.

I will find you, Serena, he repeated in his mind.

6

SERENA

Serena sat down on a settee in a pretty anteroom on the *Stargazer II*. A private valet had fetched her from the PostHaste shuttle and brought her directly here, bypassing the main corridor altogether, for which Serena was grateful.

Now he stood by the door, as if he were guarding her, while she looked around at the holo-paintings on the walls. This was clearly someone's office, someone with great taste.

She wished she could look forward to her visit instead of feeling torn apart with emotion over her recent breakup, and last night's one-night stand.

Her life suddenly seemed like a whirlwind. And she was so hungry and so nauseous at the same time. Like a physical reaction to her life spinning out of control.

Probably her blood sugar was just low. She made a note to grab a protein pack as soon as she was settled in.

The door opened.

"Ambassador Scott," a blonde woman said in a friendly way as she stepped inside. "I hope I haven't kept you waiting very long."

"No, no," Serena said. "I just sat down."

"We're honored to have you onboard, I'm Captain Nilsson," the woman said. "But please, call me Anna."

"Pleased to meet you," Serena replied.

"My partners and I own the *Stargazer II*," Anna said. "We all hope that you will have a safe and enjoyable journey."

"Thank you," Serena said, waiting for the other shoe to drop. She felt sorry for the ship owner, really. It couldn't be easy to have a pariah like Serena onboard.

"We were very sorry to hear that your... companion will not be accompanying you," Anna said carefully.

Companion. How about my louse of an ex-fiancé?

"Given the circumstances, we made some adjustments that we hope will make your stay more comfortable," Anna continued.

Serena hoped furiously that they hadn't made her give up the honeymoon suite. She'd been seriously looking forward to a soak in the heart-shaped tub from the brochure.

A hover-bot sailed in with a tray and placed it on the side table next to Serena. On it sat a steaming pot of tea and a plate of round pink things that looked like tiny cakes.

"Please, help yourself," Anna said, indicating the tray.

Serena grabbed one of the cakes and took a big bite.

She was probably being rude by not demurring, or at least grabbing a plate and a napkin, but she was absolutely ravenous.

The sugary confection melted in her mouth.

"I'm so sorry," she murmured around the cake. "I missed dinner last night."

Anna just nodded at her, slightly wide-eyed, as she shoved the rest of the cake in her mouth.

"At any rate, you'll keep the honeymoon suite, of

course," Anna said kindly. "But we took the study and made it a guard's room with a separate entrance, so that you can have accompaniment."

"Mmm," Serena nodded, munching on a second cake as she poured herself a piping mug of tea.

It was a good idea for her to have a live-in guard right now, after all she'd been through. It was entirely possible that someone would try to make trouble, especially if the ship was already carrying passengers from certain locations.

"I'm sure you're wondering if we have a Cerulean population onboard right now," Anna said, as if reading her thoughts. "And we do. Therefore, we've brought on an expert private security officer just for you. We want to ensure that you feel safe and happy throughout your time with us. Of course there will be no added charge for this service."

"Thank you," Serena said with feeling. She managed to stop eating and grabbed a napkin to wipe her lips.

"You are still on the honeymoon itinerary, so you'll have an extra spot for many of your booked activities," Anna went on. "Those are all pre-paid and non-refundable. But you can always substitute a guest of your choosing if you decide not to cancel. So if you make friends along the way, and we hope you do, you are most welcome to have them accompany you."

Serena nodded, suddenly unable to speak.

The cakes were suddenly not agreeing with her stomach. She knew that dealing with this whole situation was going to be tough, but she'd thought she had braced herself for it. It felt like her belly was a ship on a boiling sea.

She choked down a gulp of hot tea to steady it.

There was a tap on the door.

"Oh this must be your private security officer," Anna said, hopping up.

Serena hopped up too, hoping that if she moved around a little, she might feel better.

She had just fully straightened when Anna threw the door open.

A huge male body was silhouetted in the light from the hallway. He had wide shoulders and narrow hips. And a set of fierce-looking horns curved back from his forehead.

Her heart stuttered.

He took a step toward her, wonder in his eyes.

Oz...

The air between them sizzled.

Serena opened her mouth to say something.

And then projectile vomited a spray of pink all over him.

7

OZMARCK

O z froze in place, overcome with emotion, and covered in some bright pink, regurgitated substance he couldn't quite identify. It didn't matter.

Serena was here.

And she was carrying his child.

A wave of love wrapped around him, threatening to drown him in his own joy.

But Serena only gaped at him in horror, clearly feeling embarrassed for being sick.

Little did she know, she could not have made him happier.

"Oh dear," Anna said, frowning.

He knew Anna a bit form his previous time on the Stargazer II, and she wasn't the squeamish type. She was probably more concerned with how she was going to get the mess out of the carpets.

"I'll get her to her rooms," Oz said. "Send for the doctor?"

"Of course," Anna replied.

She tapped the comm unit on her wrist as he wiped his face with his sleeve and stepped closer to his mate. He certainly hadn't been expecting Serena to be his new client, but it looked like fate wasn't done with them just yet.

"I'm so sorry," Serena breathed.

"You're fine," Oz said. "I'm going to carry you, okay?"

She didn't answer, but she also didn't argue when he lifted her into his arms.

As soon as her soft form pressed against him, the mating thrall began to tug at him once more. He had to get her alone, had to talk to her...

He burst into the main corridor and ran for the platform that would bring them to her private rooms.

"Hey," someone shouted as he ran past. "Hey, that's Serena Scott."

Shit.

In his haste, he had forgotten that his client had celebrity status and was supposed to use the back halls. It was a rookie mistake, and one he never would have made under any other circumstances.

More shouts sounded behind him, followed by footsteps running after them.

Serena buried her face in his chest.

He pushed himself to the limit and made it to her platform, slamming his palm down on the sensor and praying they had already set it up to allow him access.

"Honeymoon suite," he gasped.

The platform jerked to life, sailing skyward as the assailants shouted their displeasure from below.

"Th-thank you," Serena whispered. "They hate me. Everyone hates me."

"I don't hate you," he told her tenderly.

"Even though I threw up on you?"

"Especially because you threw up on me," he told her. "Oh Serena, I can't believe I found you again."

"I know," she muttered. "I can't even get a one-night stand right."

Ouch.

He reminded himself that she did not know his people, and probably didn't know why she felt the way she did about him.

She doesn't know why her heart felt like it was breaking all day. She must be terrified.

"You're having a hard day," he told her gently. "Let's get you comfortable."

The platform came to stop.

"I'm a mess," she moaned.

"Not for long," he told her. "I'm here."

He strode to her door and placed his palm against the sensor.

It swung open to reveal a beautiful stateroom bathed in soft light and swathed in white frilly things.

From the breathy movement of the portal curtains under the air vents, to the canopy of the bed, to the soft drexxan fur rug on the marble floor, the space was a study in white.

"It's like a cloud," Serena murmured.

"It's very pretty," Oz agreed.

"And I'm going to throw up all over it," Serena said sadly.

Oz moved quickly but smoothly to the washroom and placed her carefully on the floor, where she knelt by the toilet.

"You're okay." He moved behind her, swept her hair off her neck. "I've got you."

She retched twice but nothing came up.

"This is so gross," she said.

"It's the most beautiful thing I've ever seen," he told her honestly.

She was shivering now.

"Let's get you in the bath," he suggested. "You'll feel better in the warm water with a cup of honeyed tea."

"Why are you being so nice to me?" she asked in a grumpy way.

He smiled, undeterred. "Because that's my job," he told her. "Let's get you out of those clothes."

He helped her peel off her clothing, which was saturated with the pink liquid. Then he stripped out of his own.

He took both bundles of clothing and stuffed them in the chute.

"Tea," he told the box by the door.

"My clothes," she murmured.

"The droids will launder them and bring them back," he told her. "Let's get you into the water."

He tried not to notice her supple curves, her round breasts, the swirl of her hair down her back, as he helped her into the little hot spring tub.

"Ahh," she said appreciatively as she sank into the steamy bath.

The little hot spring was almost large enough for swimming, but warm enough that the user wouldn't want to.

He stepped in carefully, relishing the heat and the feeling of sharing the water with her.

"Let me help you with your hair," he told her, squeezing a little product onto his palms.

She allowed him to bathe her as she half-floated in the water.

Oz's body was bursting as he slid soapy palms through her silky hair, and then slowly, slowly over her body.

Soon her breathing was deeper, and her sweet nipples stiffened.

"I don't understand," she murmured. "If I'm sick, why does this feel so good?"

"I'll tell you everything, but first let me please you," he murmured into the nape of her neck.

She didn't say anything, but she allowed him to smooth his hands over her belly and slide against her swollen sex.

His cock throbbed against her posterior, desperate to enter. But he focused on her, caressing her breasts with the hand that held her tight to him, strumming her sex with the other.

"Oz," she whimpered.

He circled her clitoris with his thumb and felt her shiver out a climax.

"Better?" he asked her.

She spun around in his arms, pressing her breasts to his chest, clearly ready for him to be inside her.

"First we need to talk," he told her, battling his own need, unsure how long he could hold out.

"What do you want to talk about?" she asked him, her eyes hazy with need.

"Let's get out first," he said, hoping that getting some clothes on her would help with his self-control. "We'll get you into bed, then I'll explain."

She looked disappointed, but she didn't fight him.

They got out and he helped her dry off, then wrapped them each in a fluffy bathrobe.

He grabbed the steaming mug of honeyed tea from the box on the way back to the bedroom.

When she was settled in, leaning against the headboard, he handed it to her, then crawled in beside her.

Serena lifted the tea to her lips, swallowed and then

smiled at him. "Thank you," she said. "I'm very sorry that I threw up on you."

Well, this was as good an opener as any.

"Did you know that where I come from, that's called a Maltaffian baby shower?" he asked.

"I didn't," she said. "But that doesn't make it any less upsetting."

"As a matter of fact, it does," he told her. "I'm about to tell you some things that are... a pretty big deal. I want you to know that I'm here for you. No matter how you react, no matter how you feel, I'm here to help."

"Oh-kay," she said slowly.

"I hope this doesn't come off the wrong way, but let's start with last night," he began. "You don't strike me as the type of person who has a lot of random one-night stands."

"As a matter of fact, that was my first," she admitted.

His heart sang. He knew it might be chauvinistic, but he was glad she hadn't chosen to share her body all over the galaxy, that he was special.

"I'm not fond of one-nights stands myself," he told her honestly. "But last night wasn't a one-night stand. It was something very special."

"A two-night stand?" she joked weakly, gesturing to the two of them in bed.

He chuckled. "Much nicer than that," he said. "When my people mate, it's for life. We find our match, and we have each other's backs, forever."

She blinked up at him.

"Serena, you are the one for me," he told her solemnly. "You are my mate. This isn't just for a few nights. I am yours forever."

She opened her mouth and closed it again.

She wasn't arguing.

Which meant she felt it, she knew it to be true.

"And there's more," he told her. "Our bond must be exceptionally strong. This is truly a rare thing. But there's something I need to tell you..."

He tried to find the words to help her understand that her whole world was about to change.

"*A Maltaffian baby shower...*" she murmured.

She was a smart one.

He nodded and slowly extended a hand to rest on her belly.

"Really?" she asked him, her expression becoming unreadable.

"Definitely," he told her.

8

SERENA

Serena looked down at Oz's big hand on her belly.

Her tummy had never been flat, and it certainly didn't seem any different today than it had been yesterday.

And she no longer felt nauseated.

She felt hungry.

"What's wrong?" he asked. "Talk to me."

She shook her head, unable to separate her thoughts.

She'd been left at the altar. She was over thirty. She had spent the last week mourning quietly over the seemingly inevitable fact that she would never be a mother.

It seemed impossible that after one reckless night, she was bonded to a mate and pregnant with his child.

She had been sick all over everything - that much was true. But even that didn't make sense.

"It's too fast," she said out loud. "I wouldn't have morning sickness the next day."

"It would be far too fast for a typical human pregnancy," he agreed. "But as I told you, this is a rare thing. There is nothing typical about it."

"What do you mean?" she asked.

"Conditions are often extreme for my people. It would be unwise to bring a newborn into a hostile environment, so copulation is seldom successful," he told her. "But when it is, the pregnancy is substantially shorter than for humans."

"How much shorter?" she demanded, leaning forward to look him in the eyes.

"Days, normally," he said. "Usually less than a week."

A week?

She blinked at him. "That's like something out of a horror movie."

"I'm told the body adjusts," he said. "It is rare, but not unheard of. They say there is no more discomfort for a human carrying a Maltaffian than a human child. And it's over with so quickly."

"This is impossible," she said, jumping out of the bed and pacing the obnoxiously soft carpet. "I'm on birth control."

"The biology doesn't work the same way with our species," he told her, shaking his head.

Of course not.

His beautiful eyes were so mournful.

Fuck his beautiful eyes.

"You're being ridiculous," she said firmly. "I ate something bad, probably those stupid cakes. I feel much better now, and I have a lot to do. I need to get dressed."

"The ship's physician is coming," he told her calmly. "She can verify all of this for you."

"Call her off," Serena said, trying not to scream. "I need to get dressed."

"As you wish," Oz replied.

He went to the communicator and touched a button. "Postpone the in-suite physician's visit."

"It's not postponed, it's canceled," Serena practically shouted.

"Let me help you get dressed," Oz said mildly.

She scowled at him, but didn't fight him when he unlocked the big wardrobe.

Her cases had been sent ahead so that she wouldn't have to bother with them. She knew they were filled with beautiful gowns and filmy negligees, all meant to entice her wretched ex on what was supposed to be a dream honeymoon.

She selected the most businesslike dress she had with her, a dark sheath.

Oz nodded approvingly and held it for her as she pulled off her robe and slid on some undergarments.

When she took the dress, he waited as she put it on, and then helped her with the stays in the back. He stood by as she slid on a pair of cling-heels and grabbed a purse.

"I'm fine," she told him.

"I know you don't believe me about our baby," he said carefully. "But please, humor me with one thing."

"What's that?" she asked.

"Don't drink any alcohol," he said.

She laughed.

"What?" he asked.

"I'm meeting with the power elite from some of the most important places in the galaxy," she said. "How am I supposed to do that drinking fizzy pop?"

"Ask for Maltaffian moss wine," he suggested. "I'll take care of the rest."

"What even is that?" she asked.

"When you order it? A simple ginger seltzer," he told her. "If anyone else orders it, it comes with two shots of warmed vodka."

She shook her head and headed for the door.

"I'll get that for you," he said.

"Oh no, I don't need a babysitter," she said.

"Do you happen to remember what happened when I carried you through the crowd just now?" he asked. "I'm coming to protect you. And also to guide you along a corridor that isn't public."

She didn't respond.

"It is literally my job," he reminded her.

So he was going to babysit her.

Her heart thumped happily, and then she winced.

Somehow, she had managed to snag the biggest weirdo stalker type in the universe in her one attempt at a one-night stand.

And she was pretty sure she was falling for him, in spite of every sign that he was delusional.

Wasn't that just her luck?

"Fine," she said. "You can come with me, but don't cramp my style. Not a single word about turbo pregnancy or mate bonds. Got it?"

"Got it," he replied with a broad grin.

Her heart did another little flip-flop and she smiled back in spite of herself.

It was hard to imagine that only a few days ago, she was worried that her trip was going to be boring and lonely.

Oz opened the door and she took a deep, steadying breath before heading out.

9

OZMARCK

Oz looked on as Serena enjoyed exotic appetizers with an array of beings from across the system.

She had taken his news about as well as he could have expected. Now all he had to do was stay close and watch her pregnancy progress.

He figured that even if she thought he was crazy, she would keep him close for protection. Besides, when she learned how committed he was to keep up with her cravings, she wouldn't be able to resist him.

For tonight, her biggest challenge would most likely be mood swings.

Oz had never expected to be a father. Pregnancy among Maltaffians was rare, even more so for a guard, whose loyalty was soul-pledged to his client.

In this case, his soul-pledge and his mate bond were one.

Serena Scott might just be the most protected being in the universe.

At any rate, he had never paid much attention to the

grandmothers' circle when they chatted with the young women of his clan about pregnancy.

He seemed to remember that the sickness came first. Hours had passed since that stage, so Serena should be safe from further incidents.

The next phase was mostly mood swings and food cravings.

So far, she was holding up beautifully.

She told him that everyone hated her, but he could see how the group leaned in when she spoke, and how many of the ambassadors looked to Serena before responding to an idea proposed by another.

She was a born leader.

He felt very proud to have such a woman as his mate.

Oz had read her file before knowing who she was. Maltaffian guards often took anonymous clients, even if their files often made it clear who they were.

But until he'd read over it just before meeting her in person again this morning, he hadn't realized Ambassador Scott was a young woman - her file was filled with the accomplishments of someone twice her age.

He was also surprised that someone so young had managed to enact such a controversial piece of legislation. There was an occupation of Cerulean soldiers in her sector, and she had enacted a resolution to get them out.

Which, if he was being honest, wasn't a bad idea. As a guard himself, he appreciated the concept of protection. But unchecked power wasn't good for any society.

Even the Ceruleans, allegedly the most pure soldiers in the universe, could be corrupted. It was the nature of sentience to look out for number one. Given enough time, that instinct overcame even the best training and morality - especially when there was no other shoe to drop.

But the wealthy of Serena's system, and the Ceruleans themselves, had taken her stance as a threat to their way of life. The blowback had been swift, and harsh.

He wasn't surprised her wimpy fiancé had wanted out.

Oz was only glad it had happened before they met. Serena having a fiancé would not have changed the fact of their mate bond, and Oz imagined it might have made the situation mildly difficult when he took her away from the pretender to her affections.

The waiter leaned in to take Serena's drink order, and Oz held his breath.

"Maltaffian moss wine," she said casually.

Oz felt a pang of gratitude.

She winked at him from her place at the table, and he felt the blood rush to his face.

She believed him.

Or at least she was willing to humor him.

Either way, it was a show of loyalty, and he appreciated it.

He watched and tried not to listen as she continued her dinner with the dignitaries.

Part of being a Maltaffian guard was discretion. And Oz found it easiest to block out what was being said in the first place, rather than putting it behind a mental filter, though he had been trained to do so through a form of self-hypnosis, when necessary.

Instead, he tried to enjoy being in Serena's presence while his senses focused on the room, sensitive to any threat to her.

Happily, the private dining room had only two doors and there were no windows, so his task was not overly difficult.

Once the meal was over, the dignitaries rose.

He hoped to get Serena back to her suite, but there was talk of dancing.

Oz followed as few paces behind as he dared, annoyed that they would think of taking Serena into an unsecured space, but reminding himself that he mustn't let his personal feelings interfere with professional duties.

Clients took risks. They opened themselves to bad things happening. Oz made sure they never did.

He touched his wrist communicator. "I need back-up in the ballroom, please."

Anna would come through for him - she was organized and on top of things. But that wasn't the point. For all he knew, one of these fake smiles in bespoke suits that Serena was meeting with had counted on the moments needed to bring in back-up, and was planning to attack before they could arrive.

Oz couldn't risk it.

He moved to her elbow, took hold of it.

Serena turned to him, her eyes wide with surprise.

"Will you do me the honor?" he growled. "Until back-up arrives, I can't let you out of my sight."

"How delightful," she said with a pretend laugh, loud enough for the others to hear. "I've never heard of dancing as a guarding technique."

A sudden flash startled Serena, but she smiled and turned gamely to the cameras.

"Desperate times," he replied with a half-smile.

"How can I argue with that?" she asked the group.

He whisked her away, spinning them into the crowd.

"What were you thinking?" he demanded.

"I was *thinking* that I'm among my colleagues," she spat. "And I don't want to get swept off my feet like a blushing mail order bride."

"And *I* was thinking that luring you out here without back-up would have been a brilliant plan for one of your 'colleagues' to take a shot at you," he retorted.

The music pounded, and he found it hard to concentrate on awareness of threats around them when she was pressed against him so intimately.

Her breasts seemed larger now, as if they had taken on a life of their own, nearly spilling out of the gown, nipples stiff against his chest.

"I'm so hungry," she murmured, as if their argument were forgotten.

Cravings.

"What are you in the mood for?" he asked gently.

"I- I don't know," she half-moaned. "Something sweet, but salty, without too much texture."

Salted Maltaffian jam.

Thank the gods he had some in his case.

"I have something like that, back in our rooms," he told her. "Do you need to say good-bye to your colleagues?"

She shook her head, looking up at him gratefully.

"Cancel that back-up," he said into his wrist communicator.

"Copy that," Anna replied.

Serena made no protest when he wrapped an arm around her and ushered her swiftly through one of the doors that were hidden around the ballroom, and along a private corridor that led back to her rooms.

10

SERENA

Serena surveyed her room with relief in spite of the hunger pangs that threatened to split her body in half.

"Get into something more comfortable," Oz suggested. "I'll get your snack."

She headed to the mirrored wardrobe to grab her case. Comfortable clothing was a great idea. She hadn't remembered this dress being so snug when she bought it.

Her reflection caught her eye and she did a double-take.

She looked just as she had before they left, except for a small but obvious rounding of her belly.

She turned to the side, running one palm over the curve of it.

It was real. This was very real.

Emotions tugged at her heart - fear and shock, but mostly love.

"Serena?" Oz said quietly.

She turned to him, her eyes hazy with unshed tears. "It's real."

He nodded, his eyes luminous.

He was holding a large tray of fragrant hunks of bread, with a bowl of something honey-colored at the center.

"Mm," she hummed appreciatively.

He grinned and placed the tray on the bedside table. "Let's get you out of that," he suggested.

She froze in place, a wave of lust weakening her knees as he strode toward her. Her emotions were like an out of control thruster pod, bouncing from one extreme to the other. She didn't know where it would land next.

He slid a hand down her back, and she felt the stays on the dress give way. He helped her out of it, and then removed her undergarments as well.

She was shivering by the time he was finished.

"What do you need?" he asked.

She blinked at him, awash in her primal instincts. She wanted his hands and mouth on her, but she also needed desperately to eat. She wondered if there might be some way she could do both at once.

"Let's get some food in you first," he suggested.

That was probably a good idea.

She followed him mutely to the bed.

He helped her seat herself at the headboard, then sat opposite her, placing the tray of bread between them.

"This is Maltaffian salted jam," he told her. "You take a hunk of the bread and dip it in the jam. I think it will satisfy your craving, though once that happens you may experience another craving."

Serena was already dragging a warm hunk of bread through the jam.

She placed it in her mouth and closed her eyes against the pleasure of it.

"*Oh my God*," she said with her mouth full.

Oz chuckled and she didn't even mind.

She grabbed another piece of bread and noticed peripherally that Oz hadn't taken any for himself yet.

Smart.

She wasn't sure what she might have done if he'd gotten even a little bit in between her and the heavenly food he'd set before her. He was liable to lose a finger.

After a few minutes of gorging herself, Serena finally felt sated.

"Oh, that's so much better," she sighed. "Thank you."

"Should I take it away?" he asked.

She felt a roar of protest build up in her chest, but managed to squelch it just in time. "Err, maybe you'd better leave it for a little while."

He nodded, smiling at her.

She looked down at herself. "Good grief, I'm stark naked, eating in bed," she noticed out loud.

"Would you feel better if I were naked too?" he asked.

Another wave began to rise in her, blotting out all thoughts of food. He hadn't been wrong about which craving would come after she ate.

She nodded, unable to speak.

He moved off the bed and stripped.

Serena watched the movement of muscle under golden flesh.

His big body was so beautiful, so graceful, in spite of his size.

Mate... She tried out the word in her mind and found that she liked it. Both a noun and a verb, *mate* encompassed all the raw emotion she felt under his eyes.

His gaze became heated.

She held out her arms, but first he moved the tray of bread to the table beside her.

"Oz," she whimpered, needing him so much it almost frightened her.

"I'm here," he crooned, climbing back into bed, caging her head between his arms as his hips pinned hers.

She wiggled beneath him, desperate for more contact.

He leaned down to kiss her so gently that it took her breath away. She managed to relax and focus on his touch as he kissed his way down her jawline to her neck.

He growled appreciatively as he licked one of her nipples into his mouth.

Serena moaned helplessly.

His touch awakened even more desire in her now than before. Her breasts were so sensitive that the pleasure was almost like pain.

He nuzzled her belly, rubbing his rough cheek against the little bump where their baby grew.

Our baby...

When he pressed his hands on her thighs, she let them fall apart for him.

He fell on her as if he were starving, and she was a tray of bread and salted jam.

The thought made her stifle a giggle.

But the feeling of his mouth on her sex was so exquisite, that it blocked out all other thoughts. Serena lost track of her own sounds as he flicked his clever tongue against her, pushing her over the edge so quickly it didn't seem possible.

Serena's world shattered into shimmering starlight as the pleasure threatened to obliterate her entirely.

11

OZMARCK

O z reeled with need.

Serena was still pulsating with her climax, her hands reaching for him.

He crawled up to her, kissed her eyelids, her forehead.

"Please," she whimpered hotly.

He pressed his raging cock against her warm opening and Serena lifted her hips to encourage him.

Losing all resolve, he plunged into her.

The pleasure was so acute that he howled like a gryntax and thrust into her again.

Beneath him, Serena jogged her hips up, her whole body tensing.

He let go in a storm of rapid thrusts.

Her nails sank into his upper arms and he felt her whole body milking him as she climaxed again with shuddering cries.

His own climax took him instantly, and he cried out helplessly as he jetted inside her, the pleasure turning him inside out.

When the last throes of rapture subsided, he collapsed on the bed beside her, pulling her close into his arms.

She melted against him like honey.

His hand found her belly and he cradled it in his palm, his heart throbbing with love for his beautiful mate and for the life inside her.

He had no idea how they would manage a life together. Protecting her even on this cruise was already a nearly insurmountable challenge, and he could sense her determination to continue her work in spite of the fact that they were about to have a tiny baby to care for, in the midst of some very dangerous political turmoil.

But as Serena drifted to sleep in his arms, he felt the sweet weight of her trust.

She trusted him.

He had to trust her, too.

She would not let her family down, even if they were brand new to her, and she hadn't exactly asked for them.

He felt his heart rate slow to match hers as he buried his face in her fragrant hair and allowed himself to drift off to sleep.

12

SERENA

Serena awoke in the protective circle of Oz's arms.

Her stomach screamed with hunger.

She slid out of Oz's embrace. He moaned, but didn't wake.

She hopped out of bed and landed a little hard. She was probably just a little off from all the sex, her muscles loose and languid.

The tray from last night was still on the bedside table.

She took a piece of bread and slid it half-heartedly through the jam.

But the bread was cold and dry now, and the jam a little too sticky.

What she really wanted was a mug of honeyed tea and a plate of fresh fruit.

She moved to the wardrobe, wondering if it was wrong to just get dressed and go find food instead of bathing and waking Oz to accompany her.

Her reflection caught her eye again and her mouth dropped open in shock.

Instead of just a little bump, her belly was broad and

prominent. She was full out pregnant. Based on her experience with friends back at home, she would have guessed she
was maybe six months along.

Her breasts were larger and fuller than she had ever
seen them.

A dark line ran from her belly button downward.

She stepped back instinctively, hands on her belly.

The skin was taut, the roundness beneath it firm. But Oz
had been right. There was no pain.

"Amazing," she murmured.

There was a flutter of movement under her hands, like
the beginnings of a stomach cramp that didn't hurt.

"Baby," she whispered.

Her imagination traveled lightyears and back in an
instant.

What would the baby be like?

Was it a boy or a girl?

Would it have horns?

She remembered suddenly that she had refused a
doctor's appointment last night, and she felt like slapping
herself.

She tiptoed to the communicator and pressed the
button.

"How may I serve you?" a polite voice asked.

"I'd like a visit from the ship's physician, as soon as
possible, please," she said.

"Is this a medical emergency?"

"No, no, I need a check-up," she replied. "Urgently."

"I see," the man said.

Clearly, he did not see. But she didn't care.

"Also, do you have sweets for breakfast?" she asked. "I'd
like room service."

"We have early Old Earth panned cakes with maple

sap," he said. "Or delicate Vaynleeish pastries, or if you prefer, a fruit tray from Sector-12A."

"Oh, the fruit tray, please," Serena said. "And a pot of honeyed tea."

She glanced over at Oz's sleeping form.

"Better make it two," she told the communicator.

"Very good, madam. It won't be long."

She signed off and dashed to the washroom. All she had to do was freshen up and maybe take a speedy dunk in the bath and she would be ready for the doctor.

The new distribution of weight made her a little clumsier than usual, but she managed to bathe and dress just before the door chime sounded.

The bed creaked as Oz woke at the sound of the door.

"I'll get it," she called to him, heading across the room.

She had just placed her palm against the sensor when several things happened at once.

She heard Oz's heavy footsteps charging her.

The door slid open to reveal a man wearing a terrible expression, holding a bucket of something in his hands.

She felt Oz's hands on her shoulders.

"*Fuck you, bitch*," the man at the door shouted, lifting the bucket.

Then she was flying out of the way as a wave of bright blue splashed from the bucket toward her.

As she landed, just outside the line of fire, Oz slammed his palm against the door sensor and it flew shut in the man's furious face.

For a terrible moment, she stood in stunned silence.

"Good morning," Oz said lightly.

"Wh-what was that?" Serena asked, finally able to take a breath.

"That, my love, was the beginning of a change in your

security protocol," he told her as he typed something into his wrist band.

"What *is* that?" she asked, examining the blue on the floor. "It looks like... paint."

"Very blue paint," Oz said. "My guess is that someone was trying to make some kind of clumsy point about Cerulean soldiers. But I'll collect a sample for testing before we allow housekeeping to clean it up."

She watched as he strode over to his case and pulled out a vial.

"You're not freaked out by this?" she asked as he knelt over the puddle on the floor and pulled a sample.

"Of course I'm freaked out," he said, looking up at her in surprise. "Someone has just threatened my mate, the mother of my child."

His significant look at her enlarged belly made blood rush to her cheeks.

"But this is why people hire a Maltaffian guard," he said. "I know what to do. I will protect you."

"What have I done?" she sighed, leaning against the wall.

He got a strange look on his face, and then straightened, heading back to his case with the sample.

"Let's make sure this isn't toxic," he said to himself.

She watched as he removed a kit from his case and bent over it, sliding a plastic sheath over a digital wand and dipping it into the vial.

"Just paint," he said after a moment.

She nodded.

The door chimed again, and she turned on instinct to answer it.

"*No*," Oz roared.

She shrank back and couldn't help noticing the hurt expression in his eyes.

He strode to the door.

"Identify yourself," he said.

"Dr. Phalania Bryx," a female voice said. "The front desk sent me."

"I called for room service and the doctor twenty minutes ago," Serena whispered to him.

"What's the cure for Maltaffian diabetes?" Oz asked.

"There's no such thing. Maltaffian heart blood processes sugar without insulin," the voice replied indignantly. "Is this some sort of prank? This is a big ship. I have other patients to see."

But Oz already had his palm to the sensor.

"Sorry about that doc," he said. "Can't be too careful these days."

"Humph," she said, stepping in.

Serena was a little surprised to see that the doctor was about two feet tall and covered in brilliant auburn fur. She wore dark spectacles and carried a black case.

"This is my mate, Serena," Oz said. "She needs a pregnancy checkup."

"Hello," Serena said.

"Yes, yes," Dr. Bryx replied. "Have a seat."

Serena allowed herself to be examined. The doctor checked her ears, eyes and throat, then used an auto-drone to check her blood pressure and temperature.

"You might feel a pinch," the doctor said in a bored voice.

The drone pricked the pad of her left index finger and took a drop of blood, then slid a bandage over it, all before she had a chance to prepare herself.

"Pregnancy appears to be progressing normally," the

doctor said, reviewing the screen in her hand that must have instantly processed the sample. "When did this happen?"

She looked up, sweeping a handful of fur from her face to reveal a dark, lovely eye.

"Um two days ago," Serena said.

"Not long, not long at all," the doctor nodded, looking pleased. "The bond must be strong."

"What does that have to do with anything?" Serena asked.

Oz turned away, but she saw the smile he was trying to hide from her.

"In a Maltaffian pregnancy, the mate bond is crucial to prenatal development," the doctor explained. "Maltaffia is a naturally harsh environment. Few females achieve pregnancy and even fewer complete gestation. Two adults to protect and provide for a baby are absolutely necessary for the newborn's survival. We believe that this is the reason the mate bond goes hand in hand with prenatal health."

"What happens if there isn't a strong mate bond?" Serena asked.

"Lucky for you, you won't have to find out," the doctor said with a grim smile. "Eat plenty, rest when you're tired. And be sensible."

"Of course," Serena said automatically.

"You're saying *of course* but I can see you're redecorating," Dr. Bryx said, indicating the puddle of paint on the floor. "Don't expose yourself to chemicals at this time. You're only going to be pregnant a few more days. I think you can pick your paint colors next week, don't you?"

"Oh, but that's—" Serena began.

"Thank you, doctor, thank you so much," Oz interrupted. "Maybe you'll be present for the birth?"

"My fee is fourteen thousand credits, payable up front,"

the doctor said firmly.

"Done," Oz said, touching the band at his wrist.

The doctor's screen lit up.

"Excellent," she said, smiling for the first time since she'd arrived. "I'll see you in a few days."

Oz led her around the paint puddle to the door.

"We'll see you then," he said politely.

Serena waited until the door slid shut again.

"What was that about?" she asked.

"If you want the ship's physician to attend you in the birth, we may not want to tell her you're the target of terroristic threats," he said. "Ship security is coming with your fruit tray and to take statement."

"I'm not hungry anymore," Serena said in the most dignified voice she could muster.

Her stomach chose that exact moment to growl like a wildcat.

"Are you okay?" Oz asked her.

She shrugged.

She was bringing a child into a world where people wanted to scream and throw paint on her.

And she was bringing that child into the world *this week*.

And her mate was in full military mode.

She bit her lower lip, willing herself not to cry.

"Hey," he said gently. "Hey."

He strode over and wrapped his arms around her.

All at once her troubles seemed to recede.

"I'm sorry if I'm all business," he said after a moment. "It's how I react when I'm scared. You're my mate, I want to protect you."

"Thank you," she said into his chest, unwilling to let go long enough to meet his eyes.

There was a chime at the door.

"I'm going to answer that," he said. "Why don't you hop in bed? If they have questions for you, we can answer from there. We can't have you on your feet for too long."

The feel of his hand stroking her tummy was so delicious she nearly purred.

Deep inside her belly, she felt the baby move, as if it were stroking him back.

Oz gasped.

The door chimed again.

He kissed the top of her head and waited while she climbed in bed.

"Who is it?" His voice was hard as flint again as he addressed the screen.

"Onboard security," a refined voice replied.

"Employee number?" Oz asked.

"Really?"

"You can tell it to me, or you can scream it into the void when I toss you out the nearest airlock," Oz spat.

"Seven-oh-seven," the guard replied.

Oz lifted his wrist to his mouth. "Anna, can you confirm the employee number of the security head you sent?"

There was a pause and then a crackle. "Seven-oh-seven" she said.

"Copy that," Oz said, touching his wrist again.

He placed a palm against the sensor and the door slid open.

Serena gasped when she saw the man on the other side.

He was tall with long dark hair and a beard.

And his skin was Cerulean blue, not at all unlike the paint that still pooled on the floor.

"What the fuck is this?" Oz demanded, sliding an electrified blade out of his jeans and holding it up to the soldier.

"I'm the head of security on this shift," the Cerulean said calmly. "Please put your weapon away."

"The hells I will," Oz retorted. "Get out of here."

"I'm the head of security on this shift," the man repeated.

"Anna," Oz said into his wrist, the blade held high to prevent the Cerulean from entering. "Did you send a Cerulean here?"

"Ozmarck, you of all people know we don't discriminate here," Anna's voice came back.

"He has an obvious conflict of interest," Oz growled.

"Rex Tylarr has been a valued member of our security team since we founded this ship," Anna replied. "If you want the best, this is the best. If you want second best, by all means send him back to me."

"Gods damn it all," Oz moaned.

"It's fine," Serena murmured. "Let him stay."

Oz clicked his wrist and turned to her. "Are you sure?"

"Very sure," she said, nodding. "Please put that away."

She turned back to Rex, who deactivated his own electrified blade, making it vanish into some unseen pocket like a clever magic trick.

"It's good of you to come," Serena said politely to the Cerulean guard.

"The pleasure is mine," he said, his voice warming slightly when he addressed her. "Though I'm sorry for the reason I'm visiting. May I come in?"

"Please," Serena said, in spite of the stormy look on Oz's face.

Rex strode in and sat in the chair opposite the bed. "Are you unwell?"

"Just trying to rest up," Serena said, indicating her belly.

"Congratulations," Rex said, inclining his head.

"Thank you," she said. "But given the circumstances, it's got us both a bit on edge."

"Understood," Rex said, with a glance at Oz.

Oz froze, then finally nodded.

"What can you tell me about the incident?" he asked.

"Not much," she said. "I opened the door and he threw some paint. It all happened pretty fast."

Oz huffed out a breath as if in exasperation.

"Maybe your husband noticed more?" Rex suggested.

Husband?

She didn't feel like going through the effort of correcting him.

"She called for the doctor and for room service," Oz said. "And twenty minutes later someone rang."

"Yes, but—you don't think that's somehow related, do you?" Serena was stunned.

Rex's hands were moving on his tablet.

Clearly, he thought it was.

"So you opened the door?" he asked.

"Yes," she said. "I thought it was my breakfast."

"But it wasn't," Rex nodded. "Can you describe your assailant?"

She tried to think back. "He was male, fairly young..."

"Was he Cerulean?" Rex asked.

Serena opened her mouth and closed it again. "No."

Rex nodded and typed in a few more notes.

"He was humanoid, dark hair, blue t-shirt," Oz said matter-of-factly. "He had a green wristband and a silver hoop earring in his left ear. Cheeks were flushed so maybe high blood pressure, or hopped up on something, more likely just scared. Shoes were inexpensive and well-worn. I'd guess he's Terran, somewhere in the 14th to 16th rings."

"Wow," Serena breathed.

Rex nodded and continued typing.

"Paint tests out as just paint," Oz added. "No additives, not dangerous."

Serena gave this some thought.

"So you were attacked with blue paint," Rex said. "Either this is a message on behalf of Ceruleans, or you were meant to think of it as that."

Why would anyone try to make it look like more than it was?

It didn't make sense to Serena, but Oz nodded in agreement.

"Can you classify the typical being who would have an objection to your position on the Cerulean situation?" Rex asked.

"Well... Cerulean," Serena said, feeling terrible that she was saying it to Rex. "Or someone of great wealth, someone who feels the occupation protects their interests."

Oh. That made sense.

"Would you say your assailant fit any of those categories?" Rex asked.

She shook her head.

He nodded again. "I'll holo the paint then we'll send someone to clean it up. We'll run your husband's description through the system and find the guy. It's not like he could have gone far. Hopefully, we'll be able to get to the bottom of why he was here."

"Do you think this was just some kind of prank?" Serena asked hopefully.

"On a space cruiser in motion with top notch security?" Rex asked. "No. I do not think it was a prank. I think it was a threat. You have my promise that our entire security staff will be on high alert. We will do everything possible to assure your safety."

Oz shook his head.

Serena leaned forward and placed her hand on Rex's blue one. "Thank you for your help."

He looked up at her, nodded once more, and rose.

Oz stepped out of the way to let him pass.

As soon as the door slid shut behind Rex, Oz strode over to the bed.

Serena put her arms out and he crawled in with her, holding her close.

"It's going to be okay," he murmured, stroking her hair. "Do you want food?"

She was somehow not surprised that she was still ravenous, even after everything that had happened.

"Yes," she said emphatically, the mere thought of food making her feel more cheerful again.

He pressed a kiss to her forehead, and she immediately felt a sense of peace wash over her again.

13

OZMARCK

Oz flipped the crackling Terran bacon in the pan and smiled at Serena.

She was sitting on one of the stools at the kitchen bar, gazing dreamily at the steaming pan.

If the way to her heart was through her stomach, they were both in luck. Oz was a good cook, and he enjoyed preparing meals. He had never really had anyone else to prepare a meal for, but he couldn't help appreciating the efficiency of feeding *two* beings with the same effort it took to feed just himself.

Three beings, he corrected himself, his heart stuttering as he thought of the child who grew in Serena's expanding belly.

The doctor was right, this pregnancy was progressing quickly, even by Maltaffian standards. Their bond was strong.

"What are you thinking about?" Serena asked from her perch on the stool.

"Just thinking about how happy I am to have you and junior in my life," he told her.

"Junior?" she echoed archly.

"Well, the baby," he said.

"So we're assuming it's male?"

She was teasing him, and he knew it.

"This baby is clearly very eager to meet you," he said. "That's how I know it takes after me."

She laughed and the sound shot through him, awakening him, like rain on the parched soil of his homeworld.

It had been a long time since he had laughter in his life. His work often left him lonely and far from home. And sometimes his clients ended up being less than reputable, like that idiot king he'd just ditched before picking up Serena.

It had never been a big deal before. He just moved on to the next job.

But now he had a family. What were they going to do?

"Thank you for having my back today," Serena said. "I know I should be completely overwhelmed and scared, but... I just feel safe with you. Like I know everything will be okay now."

Pride blossomed in his chest and he was unable to speak for a moment.

He simply nodded and turned back to the bacon.

When their meal was prepared, he placed the plates on the bar and lifted his tea mug.

"To our family," he said.

"To our family," she replied, touching her mug to his.

He watched as she took a sip and then closed her eyes in ecstasy.

"Oh my God," she moaned. "This is so good."

"Honeyed tea is a specialty of mine," he told her. "And that's fortified with folic acid and heavy cream."

She took another big sip instead of answering him and he smiled approvingly.

"So is there anything you want to arrange?" He phrased the question carefully, not wanting to frighten her.

"What do you mean?" she asked, wiping the froth of tea from her lips with a napkin and grabbing a slice of bacon.

"The doctor mentioned that we can expect the baby to arrive soon," he said. "What kind of things do Terran women like to have around for babies and for themselves?"

Serena blinked. "I never really thought about it. I guess the first thing is a book."

"I don't think he will be able to read right away," Oz teased.

She gave him a look over another sip of tea.

"Makes sense," Oz admitted. "What else?"

"Diapers, blankets, baby clothing," she listed. "But, Oz..."

Her face became troubled.

"What is it?"

"I know the pregnancy is accelerated, but does that mean the baby's childhood is accelerated, too?"

He took a deep breath.

He had known the question was coming, it was a natural follow-up to all she knew so far. But he had no idea how to answer.

"I grew to maturity in about half the time it took you to do so," he told her. "But our child is not all Maltaffian. In Terran-Maltaffian gestations, the Maltaffian speed is dominant. But childhood growth expresses itself differently with different children of mixed heritage."

"So we just have to wait and see?" She looked calmer about this than he had expected.

"We just have to wait and see," he agreed.

"Okay," she said. "I can live with that. We won't be bored, will we, Oz?"

"We will never be bored," he promised her, his heart feeling lighter now that the conversation was done.

Terrans had arrived in the galaxy so much later than most other beings. But once they were on the scene, they seemed to have made a priority out of mating with every species with whom they were even remotely compatible.

He realized that maybe he shouldn't have been so surprised that Serena took the news about the pregnancy and gestation with relative ease. Terrans were adaptable in ways he was only beginning to understand.

"We'll put together a list and see if we can arrange for someone to do a little shopping for us," he suggested.

Serena nodded, looking sadly down at her plate.

It was completely empty.

He chuckled and spooned his own breakfast onto her plate. "Eat this while I fix more."

Her eyes lit up and she got right to work cleaning her plate again.

Oz hummed an upbeat Maltaffian sailing song as he opened the fresher to consider what to cook next.

14

RAMM

A mbassador Ramm Vox observed the holo-images of his ex-fiancée with disgust.

Serena was wearing a simple sheath dress instead of a gown. She had forgotten her spectacles, and was grinning like a Zimbithian school girl at the brute Maltaffian who was meant to be her bodyguard, not her dance partner.

But the worst part was her belly.

Ramm squinted his eyes to be sure, but it wasn't even necessary to rotate the image to see what was right before him.

Serena was pregnant.

Ramm sighed and picked at the cuticle of his left thumb - a dreadful habit, but one he couldn't seem to shake in times of stress. He wouldn't bite it though, at least not in front of the paparazzo idiot standing in front of him, panting like a spaniel waiting for a treat.

"I assume you have the requisite documentation?" Ramm asked in the most bored voice he could muster.

"Of-of course, Ambassador Vox," the idiot replied. "It's all been sent to you in a sealed e-box."

"You digitized the verification?" Ramm spat.

"Always do," the idiot said proudly, not realizing that Ramm was angry. "Makes it easier to secure your records permanently, and database file them, should you ever need to retrieve them."

So the pregnancy was on record. Not that he would have really thought it could be kept quiet. After all, she'd been dancing on a packed dance floor on a space cruiser.

"Very well," Ramm said, touching his wrist sensor. "The customary fee has been dispatched to your employer."

The dummy blinked at him for a moment, as if he had expected a tip, or maybe a pat on the head.

Ramm turned on his heel and looked out the window until he heard soft footsteps retreating from the room. He strode back to the door and closed it, then sat at his desk to think.

He had broken things off with Serena because of her stance on Cerulean occupation. She might actually be right, but it was practically political suicide to say so at this point. And Ramm was having enough trouble with his constituency as it was.

But this...

Ramm had obviously impregnated her during their time together, a miracle given their infrequent sexual encounters. And now it looked like he had left her to be an unwed mother to his child.

The optics were terrible.

This seemingly boorish behavior was worse than requesting an end to Cerulean occupation. At least, it would be seen that way by his wealthy, ultra-conservative constituents.

Of course they wouldn't care that he hadn't known.
Which raised another question. Why hadn't the little pig
told him she was knocked up?

His thumb arrived in his mouth without warning, where
he tore mercilessly at the offending cuticle with his teeth as
he tried to think.

"You have to get her back, Ramm," he muttered to
himself as he gnawed on his thumb. "That's a no-brainer.
But then what?"

He cringed, thinking about how he was supposed to be
married to a woman who wanted the Ceruleans out of
Terran sectors.

But he certainly couldn't let her float around as a single
mother. Everyone would think he was a monster...

Maybe he could convince her to change her mind about
the Ceruleans.

But before the thought was fully formed, he knew it was
useless. Serena was obstinate as a mule. She would never let
go of this issue, and God help him if he tried to convince
her. It would be hell to be her husband in those circumstances.

It honestly would be hell to be her husband anyway.

They had started off their relationship sharing their love
of politics and community, and of course each of them was
aiming to do great things. Serena's reach to the end districts
certainly made her more attractive in Ramm's eyes.

But the love between them personally was always a
little... lacking for Ramm's tastes.

He had been raised in a home where women focused on
loving their family and not on political arguments. Ramm's
mother had stayed home to program the droids and arrange
Agro and Commute for the family, and—

Oh.

His thumb dropped out of his mouth as it hit him.

What if he could convince Serena to stay home with the whelp? She would have to leave the Parliament, and he could make noises about not stepping on her legislature for her comeback if she asked him to introduce that pesky bill.

They might start off saying she would work again when the little one was in school, but in Ramm's experience, inertia was typically sufficient to keep an unemployed person unemployed.

"She'll never agree to it," he muttered, remembering who he was dealing with.

But then it occurred to him that she wouldn't have to agree to it.

At least not right away.

He would set the bait by dangling her pet project.

Then he would close the trap on her as soon as the babe was born. She'd be exhausted from the lack of sleep and sick with love for the child. And if she wasn't, a little sedative in her coffee would do the trick.

Satisfied with his brilliant logic and the elegant simplicity of his plan, Ramm touched the communicator code on his wrist.

15

SERENA

Serena lay on the soft bed, half dozing as Oz bathed.

After an incredible five-course breakfast and a massage from her doting mate, she felt warm and peaceful all over.

When her communicator dinged, she startled into a seated position.

At least she tried.

Her belly was so large she found herself rolling backward again before she could make it all the way up.

"Good grief," she muttered, touching her wrist and rolling onto her side.

She realized too late that the tone was a special one.

The outrageously patriotic and slightly problematic lyrics of Terra-40's *Bright Eyes* signaled that her ex-fiancé was calling.

And she had just picked up.

She managed to prop herself up slightly before his image sprung to life over her wrist.

The blankets likely covered her condition, but now that he could see her, there was no point trying to adjust them.

"Ramm," she said, trying and failing to imagine why he would call.

His only good-bye to her when he left her at the altar two weeks ago was an e-box note that said simply:

IT'S NOT GOING to work.
 Best,
 Ambassador Ramm Vox

"SERENA," he purred, smiling the way he always smiled at his least favorite petitioners. "How *are* you?"

"I'm well, thank you. How are you?" she replied with a big, fake smile of her own.

Two could play at this game.

"Serena, I made a mistake," he said quietly.

She blinked at him, completely thunderstruck.

Ramm Vox *never* admitted to a mistake.

"I was afraid," he went on. "Marriage is a big commitment, and I just got a little case of cold feet. But I've regretted it every day since."

"Really?" Serena asked.

She had felt rejected and inconsolable for about a day after she got the message, and then as time passed, she realized she felt nothing more than relief.

Her relationship with Ramm had felt right for all the wrong reasons. He understood her career demands, and he shared her passion for politics.

But there had never been any real warmth between them.

It would have been a marriage of companionship, convenience and... well, political influence.

But then all the old worlds had been built on sacrificing women to loveless marriages in order to secure alliances.

And Ramm certainly could have helped her end the Cerulean occupation.

"Say something, Serena, please," he implored.

"Ramm, it's too late," she said at last. "And I think it's for the best. When you meet the right woman, you won't be afraid."

"I'm not afraid," he said quickly. "I'm only afraid that you won't come back. That we'll lose all we've worked for."

"What do you mean?" she asked.

He frowned. "You clearly haven't got a team watching polling numbers."

"You know I don't," she said. "And I'm on an intergalactic flight, so it's not exactly what I'm focusing on at the moment."

"Well, your numbers have dropped," he said, with a strange expression.

"Why?" she asked, dumbfounded. Her own constituency hadn't been wild about her allying with a snooty Terra-40 leader like Ramm. They should have been pleased about the break-up.

"So have mine," he told her.

She blinked at him.

"Come home, Serena," he said. "I'll send a PostHaste for you. Come back and we'll unite our forces. We'll have a Parliamentary majority. We can end the Cerulean occupation."

She stared at him, and he looked back at her.

He was serious.

"I thought you didn't want that," she said.

He looked down at his hands, then back up at her. "I've had a lot of time to think since you've been gone, Serena.

Time to think about us. And time to think about what you said. The occupation isn't good for our people. It might solve some temporary policing problems, but you're right, we can solve those on our own."

She smiled at him, her first genuine smile of the whole conversation. "I'm so glad to hear you say that, Ramm."

He smiled back, eyes twinkling. "So you'll come home?"

"I don't need to," she said. "We can unite our powers without a marriage. Together we can make it happen."

He scowled and rubbed his chin.

She could see that his left thumb was bleeding a little. He must have been biting his nails again.

He was nervous.

"Ramm, are you okay?" she asked.

"I need you, Serena," he whined. "I love you, and I need you. I don't understand why you won't give me another chance. You need me, too."

"I do need you," she replied, meaning to tell him she needed his political support, but she didn't need him in a personal way, not anymore.

But she suddenly realized the sound of the waterfall in the wash room had stopped.

She turned, but there was no sign of Oz. He was probably still dressing.

"Listen, Ramm, I've got to go," she said. "But I'm very excited about our legislation. Let's get together right away when I'm back."

She touched her communicator before he could argue.

Then she fell back against her pillow and rubbed one palm over her vast belly.

"I'm going to bring you into a better world than the one I grew up in," she promised the baby.

16

OZMARCK

O z leaned against the door, his strength sapped in the wake of what he had just heard.

All his joy and buoyant happiness brought down low by a few words.

You need me too.

I do need you.

And maybe it was true.

Maybe there was more to Serena's life than happiness for herself.

For a person like Serena, who had given her life to public service, maybe passing a bill would be more meaningful than anything Oz could offer her.

I can't offer her anything, he admitted to himself.

His own career was built on dangerous travel.

Right now, in their little bubble, his job was to protect her. But when they needed credits again, he would have to leave her and the child, and put himself in harm's way - soul pledged to serve his next client until his contract was up.

He clenched his fists, wishing he could break something.

He was ready to knock down a wall with this fury that overran him.

Why did some beings have full lives, lives that mattered, and others lived only to grovel?

That's what she's trying to fix.

But our baby...

And though it should have made him happy, it saddened him to think that he had chained her to him with his seed.

They were bound together now by the baby.

Bound...

Something terrible occurred to him.

He pushed off the door and paced back toward the bathing pond, frantic to move.

But he could not escape his own thoughts, they came to him unbidden.

The baby needs our mate bond. Even at this stage, if there is no mate bond, there will be no baby.

He couldn't abandon her, he just couldn't.

And even if he wanted that, how could he choose to leave her and risk the baby's health?

So that generations of other people's babies can live free of occupation.

He sank to his knees on the grasses and buried his face in his hands.

17

SERENA

S erena awoke feeling stiff and overheated.

She stretched as she opened her eyes, wondering how long Oz had let her nap.

He wasn't in the room with her anymore.

She wondered if he had run to get more food.

She decided to get up and stretch her legs. But when she pulled off the blankets, she was frozen with surprise.

Her belly was enormous.

She eased herself out of bed as quickly as she dared and moved to the mirrored wardrobe.

The startled looking woman gazing back at her looked at least eight months pregnant, maybe more...

"Oz," she called.

But there was no answer.

Where was he?

At this rate, she might be in labor before he came back.

She ambled back to the bed to grab her communicator band that she'd left on the bedside table.

A note lay beside it.

She grabbed for it, telling herself everything was fine, even as her heart sank.

Serena,

   I love you more than you will ever know.

   But I have been selfish.

   Your destiny is more important than my love.

   Without our bond, the pregnancy will disappear. You will be free to go back to your people and accomplish all the good you intend to do for them, and for the universe.

   I will never love another.

   But I am letting you go with a light heart, knowing everything that awaits you in your brilliant future.

   -Oz

Serena sobbed in a ragged breath and then screamed it out, crumpling the note in her hand as she cried.

   Fuck these stupid little men, and their stupid little notes.

   The rage at his selfishness washed away as she took in the full meaning of his message. She dropped the crumpled note to place both hands on her belly, where she could feel the life within her.

   "I am having this baby," she said out loud. "Do you hear me, baby? Don't you dare even *think* about disappearing. We are in this together, and I don't care if I have to catch him in a net and keep him behind bars to extend the bond, you *will* be born before I let him go."

   But realistically she had no idea where he had gone, or how long she had to get him back. The ship was enormous...

   It hit her that the doctor might be able to help.

She hit the room communicator and called up the holo directory.

A few minutes later a tone told her she was being connected.

"Dr. Phalania Bryx," the doctor said in a bored voice as her small, furry form appears in the hologram.

"Oh, thank goodness, doctor," Serena sighed. "I need your help."

"Dear lord, look at you," the doctor said, swiping the fur out of her dark eye to get a better look. "You're progressing very quickly, but you don't need me quite yet."

"No, no, not for the delivery," Serena said. "It's Oz, he's gone."

"Gone?" the doctor sounded shocked. "Where the hell would he go? You're about to go into labor."

"He left a note," Serena said. "Something about not wanting to mess up my future. Anyway, he said that if he left the baby would disappear. I can't lose this baby. Please...help me."

The tears that had been threatening burst from her eyes and for a moment Serena couldn't even see the holo image before her.

She wiped her eyes and looked up.

The doctor looked furious. "First of all, that was an exceptionally cruel thing he did to you. Secondly, he's dead wrong. You're far enough along, and you're human, not Maltaffian. Most likely, your gestation will simply slow to a human timeframe. Looks to me like you'll have another two to three weeks of pregnancy."

"I-I will?" Serena breathed.

"You will," the doctor said kindly. "Make sure you get your hands on ample food and vitamins. The speed of the pregnancy so far will take its toll without him there, so you need to take good care of yourself."

"Of course," Serena said.

"Not *of course*," the doctor said. "Really. Order in the supplies right away. I'm going to dial in a prescription for you, so I know you're getting the supplements you need. And try to get some rest."

"Yes," Serena agreed. "I will. Thank you again, Doctor."

"I've been pre-paid, and your lousy ex got you a great deal," the doctor said wryly. "I charged based on the expectation of having a client for a week, tops."

"I would understand if you wanted to—" Serena began.

"Don't be silly," the doctor cut her off. "I'm happy to help."

The transmission ended.

Serena took a deep breath and stroked her belly in a calming way.

"We're going to be okay," she told the baby. "And we have a little time."

18

OZMARCK

O z strode into the seediest bar the luxury cruiser had to offer.

He wasn't accustomed to drowning his sorrows in drink, but somehow, he couldn't bear to be alone.

Here, in the shadows of the below deck bar, he hoped to begin his new life, at least until he could get off the ship at the next port and find real work.

It would be exactly the same as his old life on paper, but with the realization of everything he could have had.

It would be a life spent in the cruel net of a bond that couldn't be realized.

A vision of Serena, her belly ripe with his child, appeared behind his eyelids and he shook his head to clear it.

She was no longer his. Though he would be hers until his dying breath - perhaps beyond that, if his people's spirituality held true.

But his ethereal human mate would *get over him* as they said in the old Terran cell-films.

He approached the bar, feeling half-invisible.

"Well, it fracking didn't work," a big Cerulean with a feather earring was declaring to his two friends.

"I still don't understand what the paint was supposed to signify," one of his companions said, sliding a pair of digi-specs up his nose.

Oz's spine stiffened as he realized what they were talking about. He had better hearing than most creatures would ever suspect - it ran in his blood - but he was usually able to tune out personal conversations around him. He was glad he'd been too distracted to overlook this particular one.

He held perfectly still and listened.

"It's blue, like we're blue," the third Cerulean explained, running a hand through his blond hair. "See?"

"Well, sure, but I mean what was she supposed to think?" Digi-specs asked.

"She's supposed to think she'd better not mess with us," the blond one spat.

"I know the boss wanted to keep the heat off us," said the one with the feather. "But that's what you get for hiring a Terran to do the job of a Cerulean."

The blond and the one with the digi-specs nodded quietly. Feather was clearly their leader.

"What'll it be?" the bartender asked Oz.

"Scotch rocks," he said quietly.

To his immense relief, the Ceruleans didn't even notice him.

"So what do you think the meeting is about?" Digi-specs asked the leader.

"Boss man probably wants to plan what we're doing next," Feather shrugged.

"In the Viceroy's Suite?" Digi-specs asked, sounding impressed.

"Sure," Feather said.

Blond was too busy preening to add anything.

"We probably ought to get up there, huh?" Digi-specs said.

Feather tossed back the rest of his drink just as the bartender slid Oz's to him.

Oz placed down a couple of credits.

"Come on," Feather said.

"Gimme a minute, I wanna give the waitress my number," Blond said.

"Her?" Feather asked, raising an eyebrow.

They all looked over at the waitress. She was very tall and shapely with a twist of tentacles clinging to a wooden dowel on top of her smooth, oval head.

"Not a chance," Feather chuckled.

"I have a chance," Blond said, his voice petulant.

"Don't be late," Feather shrugged.

Blond grinned and grabbed a napkin.

Feather strode off, Digi-specs scrambled to keep up.

Oz turned back to Blond.

This was his chance.

He watched as the idiot offered the napkin to the waitress.

She laughed at him, a hooting sound that trumpeted through the tentacles on her head.

Everyone stared at poor Blond, who scowled and marched out of the bar.

Oz waited a moment, and then followed, trying to stick to the shadows, while keeping the guy in view.

He nearly lost him after a minute, then realized the door to the restroom was swinging slightly.

Oz stepped inside on an outward swing and saw the regulation white Cerulean soldier boots just visible under a stall door.

He stepped as silently as he could into another stall and waited.

Following a Cerulean solider was dangerous business. Being seen to interfere with them in any way was practically a death sentence in some of the outer realms.

That was exactly what Serena was fighting to end.

Blond activated the disposal button and then stepped out to wash his hands. He must have noticed Oz's boots as soon as he turned around.

"Hey, who's there?" he called suddenly.

Oz concentrated on the image of the other Cerulean, the one with the digi-specs. He still had one trick up his sleeve - a secret he'd never shared with anyone. Oz's mother had been a Maltaffian, but his dad had been a shifter - it's where he inherited his excellent hearing, as well as one other important ability.

Blond's footsteps approached quickly.

Oz closed his eyes.

The door to the stall flew open.

He opened his eyes to admire his handiwork. He could see himself in the bathroom mirror opposite the stall. He was smaller than his normal stature, and his skin was a brilliant blue.

His digi-specs weren't quite the right shade of gray, but an idiot like Blond hopefully wouldn't notice.

"What the frack are you doing here?" the real Cerulean asked.

"Boss man told me to send you after a tray of desserts from the upper deck," Oz said in his best imitation of Digispecs's voice. "Seven-layer promenade tortes - and he likes them crispy."

"Seriously?" Blond asked.

Oz nodded.

"Frack, that's just like him," Blond said, rolling his eyes. "Let me know if I miss anything at the meeting, okay?"

"Sure," Oz agreed.

Blond headed out of the restroom and took off in the opposite direction of the Viceroy's Suite.

Oz hoped he would have enough time to get to the meeting and hear what he needed to hear. Seven-layer promenade cakes took a little time to make, even when they weren't crispy.

He faced the mirror again and closed his eyes.

When he opened them, he was looking at himself as Blond instead of Digi-specs.

It had been a long time since he tried his hand at shifting. His natural Maltaffian form was really quite adequate for all his needs. But every once in a while, being someone else came in handy.

The cheekbones weren't perfect, but it was the hair that stood out on the guy. He should be able to fool the others as long as he acted in character and didn't draw unneeded attention to himself.

He headed for the Viceroy's Suite as fast as he could without drawing attention to himself.

19

OZMARCK

O z slipped into the Viceroy's Suite and scanned the room for Feather and Digi-specs.

The Viceroy's Suite had once actually been used by a viceroy, according to a plaque by the door. Now the somber space with the wood wainscoting could be booked by anyone.

Feather and Digi-specs stood at attention in the back of the room.

Oz jogged over to join them, hoping his stride was typical for Blond.

"Slow down, weirdo, he's not here yet," Feather said with a smirk.

"Did she take your number?" Digi-specs asked, sliding his specs up the bridge of his nose.

"Naw," Oz said, remembering to run a hand through his hair, as he'd seen Blond do.

Feather just laughed.

The whoosh of a door opening to a sensor stopped him mid-laugh.

"I see you idiots are yukking it up in here," a smooth male voice said.

It was a familiar voice.

But Oz didn't dare turn to look at its owner. He mimicked the other two Ceruleans and hoped the real Blond was moving slowly with the dessert order, and that the upper-deck kitchens were understaffed.

Sharp footsteps passed him and then the owner of the voice turned around.

It took all Oz had not to gasp in shock.

The "boss man" in charge of terrorizing Serena was her ex-fiancé, Ramm Vox.

The voice was familiar because it was the same one Oz had heard on the hologram earlier, begging Serena to come back.

He must have used a PostHaste to make it here so quickly.

"Isn't anyone going to ask about my trip?" Ramm asked in a smooth, sarcastic tone.

"How was your trip, sir?" Feather asked.

"It was a fracking PostHaste, how do you think it was?" Ramm spat back. "I'm exhausted boys, and I hope we can end this today, since you clearly couldn't take care of matters on your own."

Digi-specs shuffled his feet, so Oz did the same.

"What's the plan, sir?" Feather asked.

"I left her a holo message when I arrived," Ramm said. "I've asked her to meet me here. If things go as planned, I'll have three witnesses to a re-engagement pact."

Feather nodded.

A loud banging on the outer door almost made Oz jump.

Feather strode over importantly. "State your name."

"Serena Scott," yelled a very familiar voice.

Oz's heart leapt in his chest.

The door slid open to reveal his mate.

For the second time in as many minutes, Oz fought the urge to cry out.

She was deeply, wildly pregnant. The baby was practically visible through her belly even though she was swimming in a pair of Oz's sweats that he'd left in her rooms. A pair of sunglasses rested incongruously on top of her head. She clearly hadn't put much effort into her appearance.

She was the most beautiful being he had ever seen.

He clenched his fists and fought for control.

"Serena," Ramm said, both his eyebrows approaching his hairline.

Oz clearly wasn't the only one surprised by her sudden visit.

"*No*," Serena said violently. "You don't get to talk."

The whole room went silent. Even the bulbs in the ceiling were afraid to buzz.

"I don't care about any of it anymore," she went on. "I don't care about political alliances, I don't care about your support, or my career. And I sure as hell don't care about sharing my life with a man."

She stalked over to him, eyes blazing, and Ramm shrank away slightly.

"If the universe is ready for my politics, I won't need your help with them," she said with quiet conviction. "I have something more important in my life, now. And nothing, *I mean nothing*, will distract me from it."

Ramm opened his mouth and closed it again.

Serena turned on her heel and marched out of the room.

There was a moment of silence as the door resealed itself in her wake.

"Why are you smiling, boss man?" Feather asked, breaking the silence.

"Oh, it's time for a tweak to our plans," Ramm said quietly with a smug half-smile.

"What kind of tweak?" Feather asked.

"I think it's time for the gloves to come off," Ramm said. "We've got a murder to plan."

20

SERENA

S erena reached her room again and stormed inside.

It was cool and quiet in the Honeymoon Suite, a slight breeze from the air vents fluttering the gauzy drapes and bed canopy.

But Serena felt like she was burning inside.

The communicator pinged, signaling another call from Ramm.

She ignored it.

Furious at her ex-fiancé, even more furious at Oz, she let the hot tears fly from her eyes.

"I still have you," she told her baby, wrapping an arm around her considerable middle.

The communicator dinged again. Ramm just wouldn't take a hint.

Serena needed to find something to do to occupy her mind. She figured finding something decent to wear was as good a task as any. Oz's sweats were the only thing she had that would still fit, and she felt the waistband snug on her belly whenever she moved.

She could get some clothes, and other supplies while she was out.

She pressed the room communicator before it could ping again.

"Wardrobe station. How may I be of assistance," a cool droid voice answered.

"I need to shop for maternity and baby clothing and blankets," Serena sniffed.

"Very good," the droid said. "We're on the main level, open until twenty-two hundred hours. We accept universal credits, or ship vouchers."

"I, um, I need to keep a low profile," Serena said, trying to imagine walking the main corridor in her current get-up. She'd managed to make it down two floors to the Viceroy's Suite without attracting too much attention, but she'd used the service platform and back hall for that.

"Excellent," the droid said. "Please make your way to the service platform and I'll have an employee fetch you in a private cart."

"Thank you so much," Serena replied, feeling relieved.

"We'll have refreshments waiting, madam," the droid said, glancing at her belly in the holo.

"Thank you," Serena said.

She signed off and went to the washroom to splash a little cold water on her face.

"We can do this," she told herself and the baby, trying to ignore the ping of the communicator in the other room. "We just have to take it one step at a time."

Her reflection had swollen, red-rimmed eyes, but she looked determined and... hopeful.

Serena turned off the water and glanced longingly at the steam from the pond, but the wardrobe station would be waiting. She could take a soak later tonight.

She headed to the door, determined to keep herself busy with positive, productive preparation for the future.

She was just about to exit when the communicator dinged again.

21

OZMARCK

Oz hid in the shadows just outside the Honeymoon Suite.

Instinct had sent him running to her the moment he knew she was in danger.

He knew there would be some confusion when the Cerulean lackey returned with a tray full of unnecessary desserts, but he was pretty sure they were all too stupid to figure out what he'd done.

It didn't matter. He needed to protect his mate.

But she didn't want him, didn't want any man.

She'd been very clear about that.

He could tell she was just barely holding herself together when she'd burst into the Viceroy's Suite. He couldn't push her over the edge by throwing himself at her feet to grovel, no matter how much he wanted to.

No, he should stay close, keep watch on her and just make sure she wouldn't spot him.

If the bond strengthened because of it, she wouldn't be unhappy.

She wanted his baby.

Even if she didn't want him.

He held in a shuddering sob and tried to tell himself that she would give him a second chance one day.

The door slid open and she was there.

Her eyes were red-rimmed and swollen, but she was still the most beautiful creature he'd ever seen.

"Hello," she said, eyeing him with some alarm, but no recognition.

He was still disguised as the Cerulean, thank the gods.

"Boss man wanted me to keep an eye on you," he improvised.

"Tell the boss man I don't need a babysitter," she said. "If I see you on my tail again, I'll get out my blade. I have a license to carry."

"Where are you going?" Oz couldn't help asking.

She looked at him strangely.

"To the wardrobe station," she said. "I need some cloth-ing. Tell your boss to step off. Seriously, he's calling my room constantly. It's borderline harassment. I don't think he wants to spend the rest of the cruise inside a cell."

She turned on her heel and strode down the hallway.

He watched her until her small form disappeared around a corner.

Then he headed into her suite.

Wardrobe would take some time.

And their conversation had given him an idea.

22

RAMM

Ramm rubbed his hands together briskly and tried to decide what to do next.

"How may I assist you?" his helper droid asked politely.

"I'm trying to decide whether to have lunch before or after I kill my ex-fiancée," Ramm replied.

"Your request is at odds with my protocol," the droid replied.

Blasted droids - built by some idiot cub, lacking a sense of humor.

"Never mind," Ramm said. "I'm going to make a call. Have my lunch sent up in an hour."

"Very good sir," the droid said approvingly.

Ramm watched as it slid toward the foyer to program the room service order.

When it was gone and the door slid shut behind it, Ramm touched his wrist.

A grainy holo image appeared and a tone, indicating his call was going through.

This was Serena's last chance.

If she didn't pick up this time and cooperate, he would have no choice but to get creative.

And Ramm hated getting creative.

He had been looking forward to a little luxury on this trip, since he'd had to scramble to get on board. The least she could do was cooperate so he could have it.

He was shocked when the grainy screen slid up into an image of Serena.

"Serena," he said.

She stared back at him. Her eyes were red-rimmed and swollen, as if she had been crying.

And who could blame her? She had clearly been hiding her pregnancy from him for months. The holos the other night hadn't shown half of what was going on with her.

She must have been sweating bullets when he called off the wedding.

He wondered idly if she had been wearing girdles. That could cause a baby to be disfigured.

Fortunately, this baby wasn't going to be born, so it was a non-issue. He idly wondered if there was some way to dispose of her, but still keep the baby around. A widowed single father would play very well with his constituents. And he could just get a nanny to raise the thing.

He brushed the thoughts aside for the time being.

"What do you want?" Serena asked.

There was something off in the cadence of her voice. He had never heard her sound actually hopeless before. He liked it.

"This line isn't secure," he said coolly. "Meet me in the forest, alone. We can discuss whether we can be of any help to one another."

"I don't know," she said.

"Trust me," he told her. "I want to help. That's why I came."

She sighed, a crestfallen expression on her face.

"Fine," she said at last. "Let's get this over with."

Ramm smiled.

He couldn't have said it better himself.

23

RAMM

Ramm surveyed the forest entry with satisfaction. His men were stationed all along the trail, but none were visible from the corridor.

To anyone observing, it would simply look as if he were taking a romantic stroll with his fiancée.

He hummed a few bars of *Bright Eyes* as he took a final trek down the path to the first meadow, where a shallow grave had already been dug, and then turned back toward the entrance.

Everything was going so well.

And why shouldn't he be humming Terra-40's national anthem? What he was about to do was extremely patriotic. He was taking out a woman who was a political opponent, which made her an enemy of the people. And a pain in the ass to boot.

And he'd found the only place on the whole damned ship that wasn't under video surveillance to do it.

Soon Serena Scott would be nothing but fertilizer for the silent trees in this creepy glassed-in forest.

A hastily forged note in her quarters telling everyone

that she couldn't take the pressure anymore, combined with the emergency departure of a PostHaste shuttle, would be the icing on that particular cake.

No one at home would miss her. And no one on the ship would even bother looking for her.

He got to the bridge of the song, where the high notes always brought tears to his eyes, just as he reached the entry point again.

Serena was already standing outside the forest with a determined expression on her face.

He paused for a moment and gazed at her through the glass.

Something was different about her today.

Then he shook his head. The only things really different were her gargantuan belly and her very limited time left alive.

He plastered a lovelorn grin on his face and opened the door.

"Serena, thank you so much for coming," he sang out. "I really appreciate you giving me a second chance to have a conversation."

She eyed him suspiciously, but she nodded.

"Let's walk and talk," he suggested.

She inclined her head and he reached out to place a hand on her lower back. The expression of horror on her face was enough to make him snatch it back instantly.

"S-sorry," he stammered. "I just wanted to make sure you're okay. The footing on the path isn't the best for one in your... condition."

"Don't worry about me," she said, shrugging and looking away.

Ramm plastered the smile back on his face and mentally

congratulated himself for not winding up married to this unappreciative hag.

The trees closed in around them and there was nothing but the sound of their footsteps crunching in the leaves and his own heartbeat in his ears.

It really was quite lovely.

Ramm had taken care of problems before, it was part and parcel of belonging to a powerful political family.

He had never gotten his own hands dirty, of course, and he wasn't planning on changing that today.

But he was certainly going to be close to the action.

The thought of what had to be done turned his stomach.

But what choice did he have? He'd been forced to act quickly.

Glancing over at Serena, it seemed the baby could arrive at any moment.

How was that even possible?

At last, the light of the meadow ahead seeped into the dim trail they walked.

Serena stood up straighter and her pace became more brisk.

He trotted to keep up.

When they reached the edge of the meadow, she scanned the open space ahead.

By the rings of Cylonius, she was as suspicious as a Maltaffian guard.

Ramm glanced ahead and noted with pleasure that his men were well hidden.

An element of surprise was absolutely necessary. Though this part of the forest had no video surveillance, the sound of a gun or blaster would certainly bring attention.

His men needed to get in range to use a blade before attacking.

A flunky had been waiting to post a "closed for maintenance" sign on the forest entry as soon as Ramm and Serena disappeared down the trail. Since there was only one way into this end of the forest, they should be able to ensure they were alone.

But again, all it would take would be a single forestry worker to raise questions about the bogus sign and there would be company.

His men needed to act quickly and cleanly.

Together, Ramm and Serena stepped into the meadow and he sensed the movement to their right before he saw it.

From the darkness, a blade flashed in the air.

Suddenly, the blade stopped and its wielder flew upside down toward the center of the meadow, landing with a loud thump.

Ramm spun around, and was shocked to observe Serena.

But she was already moving, her squat form bending to kick the legs out from under her next attacker.

When the second attacker fell to the ground, she throat punched him and then grabbed the blade he'd held, brandishing it menacingly before her as she searched the meadow for another assailant.

Ramm stared at her in open amazement.

Her breasts were heaving, sweat beading on her forehead. She held the blade firmly, but her knuckles weren't white, and her expression was cool as could be.

To Ramm, she seemed almost preternaturally calm.

Another figure swung down from a tree branch and lunged for her.

Serena stepped backward, causing him to fall forward on his knees. Then she knelt down fast to elbow him in the back of the head, knocking him out cold, and taking his blade as well.

With one blade in her hand and the other in her teeth, Serena rose and spun in place, searching eagerly for the next person stupid enough to attack her.

Ramm gasped and backed toward the trail again as two more of his men approached Serena.

He looked away in horror, but not before he saw her do a forward roll between them and slash outward with both blades, taking out her opponents' Achilles tendons.

He listened to them moan as he headed for the trail.

"Where do you think you're going?" Serena asked, her voice so cold it stopped him in his tracks.

He glanced around frantically, desperate not to meet her eye.

Then he saw his salvation.

Serena had taken out his head of security with her first hit. He was still out cold on his belly at Ramm's right foot.

And Ramm could see the blaster sticking out of the back of his pants.

He had no idea Serena was so good with a blade. But he doubted she was a match for a good blaster.

24

OZMARCK

O z watched with satisfaction as Ramm took the bait.

He hadn't been sure the idiot would notice the blaster.

While Ramm fumbled for it, Oz closed his eyes and slid out of Serena's form and back into his own. It felt good, like slipping on an old, worn jacket. And he was certainly more evenly distributed. Becoming Serena, even briefly, had given him a whole new appreciation for her current condition.

Ramm rose just in time to catch the end of the shift.

"S-Serena?" he moaned.

But of course it wasn't Serena he was trying to attack. It never had been.

Oz would never have allowed any client to be in that kind of danger. And he sure as hell wouldn't allow it for his mate.

He waited patiently for the ambassador to take action.

Ramm's eyes widened.

Then, at last, he lifted the blaster and aimed it at Oz.

"I see Serena has a Maltaffian lackey to do her dirty

work now," Ramm spat. "Did you know you're heart bound to serve a woman who doesn't recognize the sovereignty of the guard class?"

"You were going to kill her," Oz said in a loud, clear voice.

"That's right, Captain Obvious," Ramm replied. "Give the big guy a little pat on the head."

"Why?" Oz asked.

"Because she's ruining the culmination of all my plans," Ramm replied. "Because she's pregnant and still uppity. Because she's a bitch."

"You can't murder someone just because they don't agree with you," Oz told him.

"Watch me," Ramm said.

"I just stopped you," Oz pointed out. "She's not even here."

"I'll catch up with her," Ramm said with a horrible smile.

"So you're still planning to kill her? Even though I just caught you red-handed?" Oz asked, raising one eyebrow.

"That part won't matter when I kill you and tell everyone you attacked us," Ramm screamed.

"Okay, that's all we needed to hear," a loud voice said from the shadows.

Security agents from the ship swarmed the meadow.

Oz watched with great satisfaction as Ramm realized that he'd been duped.

25

SERENA

Serena watched from the shadows, holding her breath until Ramm was fully restrained.

Then she ran as fast as her swollen feet would carry her heavily pregnant body.

"Serena," Oz breathed when he spotted her.

"Oz," she cried, rushing into his arms and burying her face in his chest.

"What are you doing here?" he asked, pulling her back and looking at her up and down.

He was probably amazed at how far along she was.

She was amazed herself. In her new maternity outfit she looked like fully ninety percent of her was belly.

"I had to go get maternity clothing, and some things for the baby," she explained.

"You shouldn't have left your suite," he said. "Your life was in danger."

"I had a disguise," she told him. "Anyway, while I was there, I ran into Anna Nilsson, picking up a ball gown. And she got a call on her communicator."

"Anna," Oz breathed, putting it together.

"Yes, Anna," Serena said. "Anyway, she put in an earpiece, but not before I heard part of what was going on. And I had this feeling, a feeling so horrible it was like my blood was freezing in my veins. I headed over here as fast as I could."

"Oh, Serena," he breathed. "The bond."

Could it be true? Had she felt the danger to him through their mate bond?

She looked up into his handsome face. The light from above filtered through the trees, making his horns glow slightly.

"I know you don't want to be my mate anymore," she said. "But I care about you so much. And clearly you care about me."

"I love you, Serena," he said simply. "Being your mate is all I want in the whole world. I thought you needed me to let you go, but I was wrong to ever leave you, even for a minute."

She felt the words to the core of her being.

A commotion behind them drew her attention from her mate.

She spun in time to see that Ramm had somehow broken free of the security guard who held him.

And he was brandishing a blaster.

"You don't have to do this, Ramm," Serena called to him, her voice shaking slightly. "You haven't killed anyone yet."

"Fuck you," he screamed.

Everything seemed to happen in slow motion.

She saw him squeeze the trigger.

A blast of air lifted her hair from her shoulders.

A flash of movement blocked her view.

A terrifyingly loud sound echoed through the forest.

Oz fell at her feet, just as Rex Tylarr, the Cerulean head

of ship security, tackled Ramm to the forest floor and disarmed him.

Serena felt a horrible sharp pain across her abdomen and then a strange warmth splashed her thighs.

The forest began to spin around her.

Then she was falling, falling...

26

SERENA

Serena awoke in a bright, unfamiliar room.

She blinked, trying to remember how she'd gotten there.

The whole scene flashed through her mind - the scuffle with Ramm, the blaster, Oz throwing himself in front of her to take the shot, and her body convulsing in pain as she collapsed to the forest floor.

Her hands went automatically to inspect her body.

But her tummy was smaller now, practically its normal size.

She looked down at her hands, touching her empty belly through a hospital gown.

Pain shot through her heart and she could hardly take a breath.

Oz was gone.

The baby was gone.

The baby was gone...

This was more than she could bear. Her vision began to tunnel as darkness pushed in from the edges. She closed her eyes against the agony of it all.

"Serena?" a soft voice said, bringing her back to herself.

She opened her eyes to see Dr. Bryx's small form perched on a floating platform beside the bed.

"How are you feeling?" Dr. Bryx asked. "Are you ready to meet the baby?"

"Th-the baby?" Serena echoed.

"You had a terrible shock," Dr. Bryx said. "And a very close call. But your mate put himself in harm's way to save you."

Serena nodded, her heart wrenching again at the thought of Oz.

"The bond must have expanded exponentially in that moment of thoughtless sacrifice," Dr. Bryx said, a dreamy expression in her dark eye. "I've never seen anything like it. It will be a magnificent case study."

"The bond... expanded?" Serena echoed again, trying to follow.

"Yes, dear girl," Dr. Bryx said. "The baby finished development instantly, and your water broke on the spot."

That must have been the warm gush she'd felt on her thighs as she was falling.

"You passed out from the shock," Dr. Bryx said. "At least that's what we think. Your little one was born about thirty seconds later - a big, healthy baby, everything right where it's supposed to be. Prettiest little thing you ever saw."

Happiness blossomed in Serena's heart, even over the honeyed pain of losing her mate.

"And Oz?" she asked quietly.

"I'm certainly not the prettiest little thing you ever saw," a familiar voice boomed from the doorway. "But I'm fine."

"Oz," Serena cried.

He stood in the doorway, a tiny bundle in his arms and a

large bandage on his torso. He was smiling down at her, so handsome that it hurt her heart to look at him.

"Ready to meet your daughter?" he asked.

She nodded, tears blurring her vision.

He bent over her, kissing her forehead, and then placed the warm bundle in her arms.

Serena blinked back the tears so that she could focus on the little pink-faced creature in her arms.

"She's perfect," Serena breathed.

One tiny hand escaped the blanket to reach for her mother.

Serena touched the little hand and it closed around her finger.

"This is happiness," Oz murmured, seating himself on the side of the bed with a small groan and pressing a kiss to the top of Serena's head.

Serena tucked the baby close against her chest and marveled at the heavenly smell of that tiny head.

For a long time they rested that way.

Dr. Bryx slipped out, leaving their little family alone for the first time.

"You were hurt," Serena said at last, still unable to believe what had happened.

"A minor wound," he said.

"No, that's not right," she said. "I saw it, felt it practically."

"It looked worse than it was," Oz said. "I shifted my vital organs out of the way. Ramm hit me, but he didn't kill me. Better men than him have tried. All the doctors had to do was stop the bleeding. I'll have a cool scar, that's about it."

"You did what to your organs?" she asked, not sure she'd heard him correctly.

"I have some shifter blood on my father's side," he

explained. "It means I can do some neat tricks. I'll show you later."

"Really?" Serena asked.

"Really," he nodded, kissing her head again.

"Will our daughter be able to do any of that?" Serena asked, looking down at the little head she cradled and realizing it had no horns. "She looks so... human."

"Maybe," Oz said. "The horns will come in with the teeth if they're coming in at all. If that's the case, we'll have some long nights ahead of us."

"I wouldn't mind that," Serena said, stroking an incredibly soft little cheek with the pad of her index finger as the baby nuzzled closer.

"As long as we're together, I don't mind anything," Oz admitted. "Except of course we won't always be together."

"Why not?" Serena asked, feeling panic rise in her chest.

"I'm a Maltaffian guard," he said, his voice somber. "Traveling is part of what I do. And your work is too important for you to leave it just to follow me around. Not to mention that my work is dangerous."

"You need to quit your job," she said simply. "I have more important things for you to do."

"I won't lie around and mooch off your credits, if that's what you're saying," he said defensively. "A Maltaffian pays his own debts."

"You realize you've got a lot of hang-ups we need to deal with before our daughter gets confused by them, right?" Serena asked pointedly.

He blinked at her.

"Besides, I've got a job for you and you've already earned it," she continued. "I need a head of secret service, and that's going to be you."

"All ambassadors are officially accompanied by Cerulean guards," he said automatically.

"You hear that, right?" she asked. "I know that you must know how backwards that sounds. Can you see how off-brand that would be for Serena Scott?"

He nodded slowly, clearly thinking the matter over.

"And not just you," she went on. "No jobs should be based on race. They should be based on qualifications."

"That would open up positions to other Maltaffians," he said. "Public positions, not just private guard work."

"Heart bonds should be voluntarily given," Serena said. "They should not be an economic necessity. Everyone deserves choices."

"My heart is bound to yours," he told her ardently.

She felt her cheeks go warm, though of course she knew he loved her, sure as she knew her own heart was beating.

"I love you, Oz," she told him. "And I love you too, little button."

Oz leaned in to cradle them both in his arms.

She closed her eyes, basking in the joy of it.

Oz was right. This was happiness.

27

OZMARCK

A few weeks later, Oz paced the floors of the honeymoon suite.

"Are you sure Dr. Bryx thinks this is okay?" he called through the washroom door.

"Yes," Serena sang back to him. "But you can call her yourself if you want."

He could hear the seductive rush of water.

Behind that door, his naked mate was bathing, readying herself for him.

"Are you calling?" Serena's voice was teasing.

"You know I can't call her and ask her that," Oz said, opening the door and stepping into the room.

Steam rose from the pond where Serena waited for him, her long hair wet down her back.

She gazed at him, her eyes luminous, lips parted slightly.

They had been waiting for this day for what felt like an eternity.

But as much as Oz burned for Serena, he would not touch her until Dr. Bryx said it was safe.

These last few weeks had been an exquisite torture. Oz

was satisfied to his soul to have his little family together in the privacy of their suite.

But his body was on a rack with so much close contact with Serena, knowing that acting on their attraction was forbidden.

Her body was fuller and softer now, and she was more beautiful to him than ever.

In the pond, Serena poured shampoo into her palm and applied it to her hair.

"Won't you help me, Oz?" she asked.

He watched her, mesmerized.

Surely Dr. Bryx wouldn't clear them unless she was *very* sure.

"I'm going to implode if you don't get in here and make love to me," Serena said very slowly and carefully. "Starla is having her nap. This is our chance."

Lust surged in his blood, and he peeled off his clothes as quickly as he could.

Serena eyed him hungrily.

Her proprietary gaze caused his heart to pound with need. He made his way to the water's edge, seating himself and easing his legs in.

The warm water soothed his muscles, but it was tepid compared to the white heat in Serena's eyes as she moved toward him, the water rippling around her.

He slipped in beside her and pulled her close.

Tiny waves lapped at their chests as their bodies slid together like two puzzle pieces.

Serena sighed and pressed her breasts against him, sending his libido through the stratosphere.

"Let's rinse your hair," Oz told her.

He held her by the waist and let her lean backward as if

he were dipping her in one of the ballroom dances he loved in the old cell-films.

When her hair was submerged, he swung her slowly left and right, swirling the shampoo out of her hair.

She smiled up at him, the perfect dance partner.

Her hair was still a little bubbly though, so he eased an arm around her neck to support her and used his other hand to massage her scalp, running his fingers through the silky ribbons of her hair.

She hummed in enjoyment.

"Gods, but you are beautiful," he told her.

"So are you," she told him, extending a hand to cup his jaw.

"I'm sure that's not true," he said with a grin. "It's only because you love me."

She shook her head, eyes gone dreamy. "No," she said. "Look at this handsome face that wakes me up with breakfast every morning. These strong arms that hold me."

Her hands moved over his body as she spoke and he held perfectly still, drowning in waves of need.

"And those horns," she murmured, sliding a gentle hand over his right horn and sending a jolt of lust through him.

"Enough," he groaned, lifting her in his arms and carrying her out of the pond.

"Wait, where are we going?" she moaned.

"I need to do things to you that I can't do in here," he told her.

Her pleased giggle cascaded through his senses like a waterfall.

He felt weightless as he carried her out of the washroom and into the wafting curtains that surrounded their bed.

"Oz," she murmured as he laid her down.

He covered her body with his, desperate to plunge into her and reclaim her physically.

But he had to be gentle.

And besides, this was special.

They had been in the throes of the mating thrall in the beginning. Then they had been off-limits for so long.

This was the first time they would possess each other because they chose to do so, with open eyes and open hearts. He had to make it perfect.

He leaned down to kiss her forehead, her eyelids, her cheeks.

She smiled and twined her arms around his neck.

His heart ached with the joy of it. He kissed his way down to the shell of her ear.

"I love you," he whispered, then flicked the lobe with his tongue.

Her hips quivered beneath him and he nearly lost his resolve.

He trailed kissed down her neck, and softly caressed her breasts with gentle hands.

"I can't wait until these are mine again," he murmured, nuzzling between them.

When he pressed kisses to her navel, she giggled.

"Are you ticklish?" he asked her, looking up.

"Definitely not," she said quickly.

Oh, what fun he would have with her...

But they had a lifetime for that. For now, he was desperate to please her again.

He nuzzled the tender flesh of her thighs, urging her to part them for his mouth so he could taste heaven.

28

SERENA

Serena gasped and nearly came apart at the first stroke of his clever tongue.

They had waited so long. She was sure Dr. Bryx was being overly cautious about her celebrity patient, and that they could have done this days ago.

Serena had certainly been willing to try, but Oz would have none of it.

It felt like she had suffered endless sleepless nights, his body pressed to hers, rigid as steel, her own sex swollen with need and no hope of relief.

Now he fed on her, his hungry tongue demolishing her desire to extend this pleasure.

He eased a big finger against her opening.

Serena wailed and felt herself exploding on his tongue, the bliss tearing her apart.

Oz slowed his movements, coaxed long minutes of ecstasy from her, then immediately began lapping at her again.

"Oh, no, I can't," she moaned.

But she found that she could.

The second climax was more intense than the first and she bit her lip to keep from screaming as the ecstasy was wrung from her.

"Oh, Oz," she moaned as she came down from it.

"Again," he growled against her.

The room was silent but for the sound of her own ragged breathing and then the cries he wrenched from her as he brought her to a third climax.

At last the waves of pleasure subsided and he crawled up to her, his mouth glistening with her juices.

She could feel him throbbing against her hip, so hard it seemed he must be in pain.

"Better?" he asked.

"Not yet," she said, sinking her nails into his upper arms and urging him to take her.

"We don't have to, Serena," he said, his jaw tight. "If you want a little more time, it's fine with me."

"No," she moaned.

"I don't want to hurt you," he whispered, fear in his eyes as well as lust.

"Then let me do it," she offered.

"What do you mean?" he asked.

"Roll over on your back," she said in her most commanding voice.

He smiled at her slowly, then released her and lay back, arms behind his head.

Gods, but he was gorgeous.

She soaked in the sexy smile, the broad, muscular chest, and the huge, stiff cock that pulsed for her.

She straddled him before he had a chance to change his mind, pressing her lips to his and grinding her hips downward, sliding his cock against her warm, slippery opening without allowing him to penetrate.

"Serena," he moaned into her mouth.

"Is this okay?" she whispered, mostly teasing him.

"Please," he groaned.

She took him in her hand and eased him into her.

"Ohhhhh," he moaned.

The sensation of having him inside her again was heavenly.

She moved slowly, sliding up and down the rigid length of him.

Impossibly, the wild pleasure built within her again, flames of lust threatening to consume her.

She moved faster, chasing her ecstasy.

Then one of his hands was on her hip, guiding the rhythm, as the other slid between them to toy with her clit.

Serena cried out as she splintered with pleasure again, pushed over the edge by the wild heat of him jetting into her as his climax found him.

At last it was over, and she collapsed on his chest, panting.

"You're incredible," he whispered into her hair.

"I love you, Oz," she murmured.

"I love you too, my beautiful mate," he whispered back. "And I have an important question for you."

"Can it wait until after I take a little nap?" she asked.

"Nope," he said. "But it's a quick one. Will you marry me?"

She lifted her head from his chest. "Do they even have weddings on Maltaffia?"

"No, but they do in the Terran zones," he said. "Let's honor your culture."

"Really?" she asked.

"I mean, unless you aren't sure? We can wait as long as you want," he said.

"Yes," she said quickly. "Yes, of course."

"Thank you," he said. "We'll pick out rings tomorrow, if we ever decide to leave this bed, that is."

"I hate to break it to you, lover, but Miss Starla is going to need me long before then," Serena giggled.

"Fine, she can have you," Oz allowed. "But I don't think I'm done with you quite yet."

"What?" Serena asked.

But he was already flipping her onto her back and nuzzling her neck.

And the anticipation had her shivering all over again.

29

SERENA

Serena smoothed down her skirt and sighed with pleasure.

The wardrobe station on this ship was incredible. Here she was, just weeks from giving birth, and they had crafted a wedding gown that looked absolutely beautiful and felt like a cloud.

She knew they could have waited until they reached one of their home sectors, but neither Serena nor Oz could bear to postpone the ceremony for that long.

And besides, Serena felt that each of them was secretly a little sentimental about this on-ship forest where they had declared their love and given birth to their daughter.

She glanced across the meadow to see that little Starla was snuggled in the many arms of Vaxyn, the head of the ship's spa. Vaxyn was crooning in a lovely voice as Starla opened and closed her chubby little fists.

Most of the other chairs were filled. It was going to be a relatively small ceremony, with just the ship's VIPs, who Anna hoped would befriend Serena and Oz, now that Starla was old enough to get out and about.

There were guards as well, stationed discreetly near the entrance. But they were not Cerulean guards.

All Ceruleans onboard the ship were being held in the lower deck until they reached a planet where they could be tried.

After their attack on Serena, it came to light that many of the Ceruleans onboard had either been part of the conspiracy against her, or had gotten riled up enough by it to act out in a dangerous manner. When the leaders of the ring had refused to name which Ceruleans were directly involved, the founders of the ship had been left with no choice but to place them all in holding, even Rex Tylarr, the Cerulean head of ship security who had assisted them and taken down Ramm when he'd fired on her.

She knew it was going to cause problems in the long run, but Anna and the others refused to handle it any other way, for the sake of safety. And the rule of ships-in-transit applied, so the founders' decision was binding.

Serena had every intention of seeing justice served, but for now, she tried to focus her thoughts on the wonderful day she was about to share with her new friends and family.

There was a stir among the guests as Anna Nilsson swept in with three people behind her.

"Serena, you look exquisite," Anna said. "Before the ceremony begins, I wanted you to meet Prince Zane and Princess Juno of Agwithia and their friend, Rose."

"Hello," Serena said with a smile.

She remembered hearing something about the surprise royal romance that had blossomed just before she came onboard the *Stargazer II*. They certainly seemed nice enough.

The royal couple smiled happily at her. The woman called Rose hung back slightly, looking a little nervous.

"Juno and Zane were married onboard recently too," Anna said with a sparkle in her eyes.

"I heard about that," Serena said. "Congratulations, your majesties."

She curtsied deeply.

"Thank you," Zane said. But he was looking at Juno, who squeezed his hand and smiled at Serena.

"It's true that my husband is the Crown Prince of Agwithia," Juno said. "But Rose and I are from Terra-4. That's why we asked to meet you."

"Oh," Serena said, smiling widely. "I'm very glad to meet you then. I haven't met many of my own people on this ship."

Serena herself wasn't from so far out as Terra-4, but it was still close enough to feel a kinship. And she knew Terra-4 was in a sector that was at the heart of what she was fighting for.

"We appreciate what you are doing so much," Rose said, stepping forward suddenly. "Ever since Juno and I can remember, Terra-4 has been under Cerulean occupation. If there is ever anything I can do to be of service to you, please let me know."

The girl bowed deeply, in the manner of the Terran military.

"Are you in the service?" Serena asked.

"I was, madam," Rose replied. "I finished my tour right before Juno called me to join her on the ship."

"There is something you can do for me," Serena said thoughtfully. "But only with Anna's permission."

"If you're looking for extra security just ask," Rose said passionately. "My background was mainly in Agro, but I had weapons training, just like everyone else. I would ensure no

Cerulean ever got within a hundred yards of you or your family again, if you asked."

"Oh it wouldn't be for me," Serena said. "But I'll think about it. And thank you for your kind offer."

The three wished her well and went to their seats.

Anna stayed behind.

"What would you need my permission for?" Anna asked quietly.

"It's your ship, so it's your decision," Serena said. "But I'm having a hard time sleeping knowing that Rex Tylarr, who saved my life, is being held on the lower deck with the others."

"He's a Cerulean," Anna said. "No exceptions."

"Aren't we in this mess because Ceruleans see Terrans as inferior?" Serena asked. "We need to move beyond these petty prejudices and lead by example. Besides, you and I both know he's a decent man and he's not safe down there with the others."

They had argued about this before, but Serena hoped that she now had a solution to Anna's biggest concern.

Anna frowned. "What would you want me to do with him? I can't let him free on the ship until there's been a trial."

"Why not put him under armed guard?" Serena suggested, nodding toward the woman who had just offered her services.

"Rose?" Anna asked. "Oh no, I couldn't do that. She hates Ceruleans. If you knew what life was like on Terra-4, you wouldn't ask for this, Serena."

"You're right, I don't know what life is like on Terra-4, but I hope it's about to get better," Serena said. "And if Rose can learn to get along with a Cerulean, won't that be a lesson for all our people?"

"I suppose, since she is military," Anna mused. "And Rex has a number of witnesses placing him in opposition to the attack."

Serena nodded.

"I'll think about it," Anna said. "How's that?"

"Thank you," Serena said. "Thank you so much."

Anna squeezed her hand. "My pleasure. But you'd better get back there if you want to surprise your fiancé with your dress."

"Good thinking," Serena said. "Thank you again for arranging everything."

"It was my pleasure," Anna said. "Besides, I was fresh from the last one."

"Intergalactic scavenger, ship founder, and now wedding planner," Serena teased. "What else are you going to do with your life?"

"No idea, but whatever it is, I'm game," Anna laughed. "I like to stay busy."

"Have you ever thought about intergalactic politics?" Serena asked.

"Isn't that what I already do?" Anna asked, with one eyebrow arched.

"So you really are considering what I asked about Rose and Rex?" Serena asked. "It would be a wonderful wedding gift."

"I'm thinking about it," Anna allowed. "But it's time for you to get married now."

The light was subtly shifting in the forest, showing off the fairy lights Anna and her mate, Leo, had hung earlier in the clearing.

"Thanks again," Serena called over her shoulder as she headed down the trail far enough that Oz wouldn't be able to see her.

30

OZMARCK

Oz watched from the corridor as the light source in the forest dimmed and twinkling fairy lights appeared.

He had claimed Serena as his mate the night they met.

They already had their first child.

Their fates had merged in every possible way.

But somehow, the sweetness of the Terran ritual tugged at his heart and he felt an unexpected urgency to say the words and make them belong to each other in yet another way.

Baby Starla wasn't exercising her mighty lungs, which told Oz he had a bit more waiting to do.

After all the excitement, Oz and Serena had stayed in the honeymoon suite for weeks in a bubble of love, doting on their daughter constantly.

As a result, Starla was furious whenever she wasn't tucked snugly in her mother or father's arms.

Serena and Oz had prepared each other for a very noisy wedding.

He was surprised when Anna beckoned him from the opening of the forest.

"Is she ready?" he asked.

"Sure is," Anna said. "You're not having second thoughts, are you?"

He laughed out loud. "Hell no, the opposite of that."

"Good," she said with a smile.

"What about Starla?" he asked. "Why isn't she crying?"

"Oh, you'll see," Anna said. "She's happy as a mynarr. You ready to get married?"

"Let's go," he said.

He headed to the forest, took a deep breath, and opened the door.

Anna slipped in behind him, and together they headed down the trail to the meadow.

The trees closed in overhead and he felt the peace of the forest envelop him.

Oz wasn't used to being the center of attention. Discretion and disappearing into the shadows were the hallmarks of his career. He had no idea how to stand in front of a crowd, even a small one.

But the tranquility of the ancient trees lent him a measure of strength and he walked on, knowing he was growing closer to his small family with every step.

"Do you know what she asked for as a wedding present?" Anna asked softly.

He shook his head.

"She wants me to release Rex from the lower deck and allow him freedom on the ship, under guard of course," Anna said. "She doesn't think it's fair for him to be held with the others."

"What did you say?" Oz asked, moved that even in their joy, his compassionate mate thought only of justice.

"I told her I would think about it," Anna said. "It's not so much Rex's behavior that I'm worried about. If he's allowed to be free, it might look like I'm playing favorites, or that he cut some kind of deal. And that might put him in danger."

Oz nodded.

"That makes sense," he said. "But we should judge people by their actions, not their race. Rex showed his loyalty."

"That was Serena's argument, too," Anna said.

"I'm not surprised," Oz said. "I hope you'll consider her proposal."

"So both of you are asking me for this on your wedding day?" Anna asked.

"It's better than flatware," Oz shrugged.

"Very funny," Anna said. "Here we are."

She slipped ahead of him into the meadow and sat in the last open seat.

Oz strode down the aisle, eager to be close to his mate and child once more.

Their lives together had just begun, but even an hour spent out of their company made his heart feel like it was stretched taut over the distance between them.

When he reached Leo, who stood at the edge of the meadow, holding the ship's log, he turned to face the small crowd.

In the front row, baby Starla was cradled safely in two of Vaxyn's many arms. A third arm stroked her little cheek, while a fourth tickled her belly.

Anna was right. It was no wonder Starla was content.

He smiled at Vaxyn, who nodded to him and then went back to crooning at the little one.

He could hardly blame the midnight alien for being so attentive. Everyone who saw Starla seemed to adore her. She had her mother's charisma, that much was certain.

He hoped they could raise her to have his loyalty as well.

If they succeeded, gods help any man or beast who got in her way.

Music began to play softly.

He fixed his eyes on the opening of the trail, where his Serena would emerge. Sure enough, she appeared a moment later, in a rustle of pale fabric.

He would have been overjoyed to see her if she'd been wearing a waste container. But the gown was exquisite, hugging her curves, accentuating the honeyed tone of her skin and the waves of dark hair that hung down her back.

She smiled at him and he felt like his heart would shatter.

The words of the ceremony flowed over him. He tried to remember his part without coming out of the trance of love she had put him in.

At last Leo called for him to kiss the bride.

Serena went up on her toes to meet him and he swept her off her feet, kissing her hard and long until the cheers of the crowd finally roused him, then placing her gently on the ground.

She blinked up at him, looking a little dazed. "Is it always going to be like that?" she whispered.

"Like what?" he asked.

"Dizzying," she murmured.

"I hope so," he told her. "But don't get too dizzy yet, I think these people are expecting us to dance and party with them all night."

"Well, it won't be the first time," she teased.

"And it certainly won't be the last," he replied, pressing a kiss to her forehead. "Ready to start our life together, wife?"

"Yes, my husband," she replied with a wide grin.

He grabbed her and together they headed into the crowd to collect their sweet daughter and join their new friends.

Thanks for reading Cosmic Mate!

Want to see what happens when Princess Juno's best friend, Rose, and her sworn enemy, Rex, the Cerulean soldier, get a whole lot closer than either of them ever imagined?

Are you ready for for them to be forced to work together to solve a mystery full of stolen goods, intergalactic smugglers, a mysterious creature lurking in the forest, and more romantic tension than you can fit in a luxury space cruiser?

Then keep reading fora sample of Conquered Mate: Stargazer Alien Space Cruise Brides #3!

Or just grab your copy now:
https://www.tashablack.com/sascb.html

CONQUERED MATE - SAMPLE

ROSE

Rose Mendez strode across the bustling Agro department of the *Stargazer II* luxury cruiser.

The enormous room was a study in white and green. Marble floors met ivory metal walls that rose up to a vaulted ceiling made of massive glowing solar squares.

And between the floor and ceiling, a forest of fruits and vegetables hung from clear hydroponic pods, an organized tangle of irrigation tubes threading them all together, like the blood vessels of some huge leviathan.

All around her, human and droid workers bustled to fulfill Rose's orders.

To an untrained observer, it might have seemed chaotic. But Rose had arranged every detail. To her, the room and all its inhabitants were as synchronized as the workings of a magnificent Terran grandfather clock.

"Rose," one of the new assistants called out. "Do you have a minute?"

She paused to greet the young Bergalian.

"Yes, Zyrxa?"

"Your message was to get rid of the extra carrots." Zyrxa's

furry face was a mask of confusion.

These poor newbies took everything literally.

Rose was just glad the kid had stopped to ask instead of dumping their overstock of beautifully ripe carrots. Everyone knew Rose hated waste.

"Call the chef at the Main Dining Room," Rose explained. "Let him know he can double the carrots in the salads and offer carrot cake on the dessert menu for the next month."

"Oh," Zyrxa said, looking relieved. "What if he doesn't want to?"

"Then shift the call to me," Rose said grimly.

"Thank you," Zyrxa cried, dashing off, presumably to do Rose's bidding.

The produce buyer for the Titanium Dining Room was already inside, poking around the mango tree.

Good, Rose had a plan for that.

She jogged over.

"Danla," Rose said in a cordial way.

"Hi there," Danla replied, her three ruby eyes fixed on the small grove of mango trees that were suspended from the ceiling before her. "The mangoes are coming out nicely."

Rose flushed with pleasure.

She had been working hard to cultivate the little trees.

"I have a proposal for you," Rose said.

"I'm listening," Danla told her.

"I would be willing to triple your mango share for the week," Rose said. "In exchange for three cold storage containers."

"We can't get more of those until we get to port," Danla said dismissively.

"We'll be at port soon," Rose told her. "And you can collect your produce daily in the interim if you want."

That would be a pain in the ass. Danla was known for being very particular. Sometimes it felt like she had far more than three eyes looking for faults with the fruits and vegetables. It was much easier for Rose to have her weekly containers pre-filled and waiting.

"Why do you want them?" Danla asked, looking tempted but wary.

"We have a surplus," Rose said.

"So eject it," Danla shrugged.

"I'm going to trade the best of it on Sheldrahk for seedlings," Rose said, practically hugging herself with the joy of it.

"What kind of seedlings?" Danla asked.

"Apple," Rose said.

"Like... from the Terran fairy tales?" Danla asked.

"Yes," Rose said with a grin.

"Where the hell are you going to put apple trees in here?" Danla asked, gesturing at the crowded airspace above.

"Oh, I have a plan for that," Rose told her.

"I'll bet you do," Danla said, shaking her head.

"Apple trees on the *Stargazer II*," a deep masculine voice said from behind her. "Incredible."

Rose spun around to find Leo, one of the ship's founders and co-captains, smiling down at her.

"My wife sent me to find you," he said. "Can you come with me for a few minutes, please?"

"Sure," Rose said. What choice did she have? When Anna Nilsson called, you answered. "Danla, we'll finish this conversation later, okay?"

"By all means," Danla said. "I'm looking forward to choosing my produce daily."

Rose resisted the urge to roll her eyes. She reminded

herself it would be well worth dealing with Danla to bring apples onboard.

And it sounded like she'd just made herself a deal.

"You're working very hard," Leo said politely as they headed out of Agro and into the corridor that led to the main deck.

"I enjoy my work," Rose told him honestly. "Thank you for making a place for me here."

"We seem to have nearly doubled production since you arrived," Leo said.

"Well, the old irrigation system wasn't as efficient," Rose told him.

"The engineers told me that system was the latest tech," Leo said.

"It was," Rose agreed. "But they made some changes in the new line that ended up being a big step back in a lot of ways. The older valves are much better, and easier to service. We traded our new stuff for older equipment and had credits left over for seedlings. Now we're running more efficiently *and* we have more stock."

"Incredible," Leo said again. "We're very lucky to have you onboard."

Rose grinned as the blood rushed to her cheeks. Back on Terra-4 praise at work was a rare experience.

"Here's the thing though," Leo said carefully. "I'm told we're far outproducing what we need already, with more surplus on the way."

"But that's a good thing," Rose told him, surprised at his intimation of displeasure. "We can trade our surplus for other things we want."

"But, Rose, you don't need to do that," Leo said gently.

She bit her lip.

He was trying hard not offend her by just coming out

and saying that she wasn't in some backwater outer ring settlement anymore, and she didn't need to struggle for every scrap.

She knew she didn't have to do any of the things she was doing to make the Agro department run above and beyond. But how could she not want Agro to run as productively as possible?

Back on Terra-4 there was never enough food.

Rose remembered so many hungry nights, and the struggle to make things grow when there wasn't enough light or water.

Now she had the opportunity to actually produce a surplus and enrich the ship's stores.

It felt almost criminal not to squeeze every nutrient from the amazing facility she was running.

"Besides, Anna needs your help with something else," Leo went on. "We're hoping you can take a temporary break from Agro to assist with this project."

"What kind of project?" Rose asked, trying not to wince.

She hated to have to walk away from Agro for any amount of time when she finally had things running so nicely.

"She'll explain everything," Leo said. "But it's military."

Rose nodded.

If it was relying on her military background, there wasn't much danger of her really being pulled off Agro.

Rose had finished her tour of duty in the Terran military right before her best friend Juno's husband sent a PostHaste to bring her aboard the *Stargazer II*.

She'd had the requisite combat training, but had spent most of her service time in Agro.

Whatever Anna wanted, if it was military, there was someone else more qualified onboard to take care of it.

Rex Tylarr stood in the back corner of the holding cell and watched as the guard headed out to the foyer to change shifts.

At every eight-hour shift change, there was a brief interval that left Rex alone with his cellmates for a few minutes. He wouldn't have stood for that kind of oversight when he was head of security, but that time was behind him.

He braced himself, feet shoulder width apart, calling on years of training in the Cerulean army to calm his nerves and amp up his senses.

The only trouble was that his Cerulean cellmates all had the same training.

The first one rushed him, a huge brute with a feather tattoo. His fists were like hammers, and he was fast to be so big, but Rex had learned after the first few times that he telegraphed his attacks.

Rex held on until the last pre-tooth-shattering moment and then ducked his head, causing the punch to hit the crown of his head and doing more damage to the attacker's fist than to Rex.

A knee came at his groin next and he managed to block it.

But the third hit glanced off his rib cage, practically knocking the breath out of him.

Pain blossomed, sending stars in front of his eyes.

And two more guys were already headed his way.

He managed to get the big guy in a choke-hold and held him up in front of himself like a shield as he struggled wildly, every movement an agony to Rex.

He could kill the man with no more than a harsh twist, but that wasn't really an option for Rex. He tried hard not to do much damage to any of them, it would only make things worse.

He felt the lure of the battle rage calling to him, willing him to use his innate power to defeat his foes. But he knew his attackers were holding themselves in check as well. If any one of them decided to amplify in this small cell, it would be a disaster. No, they weren't going for a kill. They wanted to make him suffer.

He was holding them off, but Rex felt himself wearing down.

"Fucking traitor," the smaller of his two assailants muttered.

Rex had been the only Cerulean onboard not to rise against Ambassador Scott during the assassination attempt.

As a matter of fact, Rex had tackled her enemy to the ground when he pulled a blaster on her.

And the only thanks he got was being jailed with the rest of the Ceruleans.

Now his countrymen wanted to hurt him with even more passion than they had wanted to kill her.

So far, they had settled for beatings, but they would tire of that soon enough.

Rex was friendless, and his days were numbered.

But he wasn't giving up.

The little guy was advancing on him, flanked by the other one.

When the smaller man took a swing at Rex's jaw, he blocked it.

But the other guy got him in the eye, opening up a nasty cut from the day before.

Hot blood gushed down his cheek.

"Hey, what's going on in here?" a familiar voice called out.

He released the big guy and all three of his attackers scrambled to blend into the rest of the group.

The security guard stepped up to the bars, a concerned look on his young face.

When Rex had been head of security, he had trained this particular guard, Jensen Wayne.

"Boss, are you okay?" Jensen asked, his voice quavering slightly.

"Fine, Jensen," Rex replied. "And I'm not your boss anymore."

"You're bleeding," Jensen pointed out.

"Yeah," Rex grunted.

"What happened?" Jensen asked.

He looked back at his attackers before answering.

"I fell," Rex said. "Hit my head on the bars."

There were snickers from the crowd of Cerulean prisoners.

It figured that they laughed at his loyalty. But he wasn't going to give them the satisfaction of tattling like a schoolboy.

"Boss, if you just say the word I can get you put in solitary," Jensen whispered. "Nobody wants them to hurt you. Ambassador Scott asks about you every day."

But the last thing Rex wanted was special treatment.

He had treated Terrans like beings with as many rights as anyone else in the system - shown them respect and dignity as individuals.

But when the shit hit the fan, they had shown him that they saw him as no more or less than one more member of his race - defined only by his blue skin and muscular form.

He wanted no favors from them.

"I said I fell," he hissed. "And I'm not your boss."

Jensen's face fell and he stepped back against the wall.

Ambassador Scott had tried sending him missives and special food in the beginning.

He sent it all back without looking at it.

He didn't regret saving her. But there was no point clinging to a connection with Terrans.

He leaned back against the wall, babying the bruised rib a little and trying to ignore the furious stares of his cellmates.

He'd gotten off relatively easy at this shift change.

He would rest up and be ready to face them again at the next one.

He was sure they would be ready to face him, too.

His injuries were beginning to add up. Sooner or later they were going to get the best of him.

"Not today," he muttered to himself. "Not today."

ROSE

Rose followed Leo to a platform and held her breath when they stepped on.

"Lower deck," he said, placing his palm on the sensor.

She had just a fraction of a second to wonder why they would be going to the lower deck.

Then the platform dropped and she was mercifully to afraid to scream as her stomach threatened to exit her body through her mouth.

After what felt like a lifetime of falling, the platform stopped abruptly.

Rose held back a gasp of relief.

"Takes some getting used to, huh?" Leo asked.

"We don't have anything like this back on Terra-4," Rose said.

"That's the fun part about a space cruiser," Leo told her. "Everyone is from someplace different. We're all getting used to something out of our comfort zones."

She smiled in spite of herself.

Leo was super nice. Anna was very lucky to have such a great partner.

Rose had spent most of her life scrambling for survival. She hadn't given a lot of thought to romantic entanglements.

But if she did one day, she hoped she could find someone half as nice as Leo. He was wonderful with their little boy, Tolstoy, and friendly with all the passengers, too.

And the love he felt for Anna was palpable every time the two of them were in a room together.

But there was no time in Rose's life for a relationship like that. She had Agro to think about now.

And deep down, she had to admit that part of the reason she was working so hard was the hope that maybe if she could create enough surplus, they would allow her to send some supplies back to Terra-4. She knew in theory that corporations sometimes gave bonuses to their best employees.

Rose was so busy fantasizing about sending containers of supplies back to Terra-4, that she failed to notice where they were going until it was too late.

Two security guards flanked a metal double door.

"Is this... the holding cell?" Rose asked.

"Sure is," Leo replied. "Thanks, boys."

The two guards opened the doors for them.

A horrible sensation crawled under Rose's skin and she felt her stomach contract.

"I didn't steal anything," she heard herself say in a hollow voice.

"What?" Leo asked.

"I would n-never steal from this ship," Rose stammered.

"Of course you wouldn't," Leo said. "You've done nothing but enrich the *Stargazer II* since you got here. Oh—oh gods, did you think I was bringing you here to arrest you? That's not it at all, Rose. I'm so sorry that my actions caused you distress. That was not my intention."

Blood rushed back to her head and she felt almost faint with relief.

Leo offered her an arm.

She shook her head, mortified.

"I have learned from Juno and Zane that things are not good for your people on Terra-4," Leo said gently. "But I'm getting the feeling that I don't fully understand how bad the situation is."

Rose nodded mutely.

The situation on her homeworld was bad enough that any Terran could be taken into Cerulean custody at any time, for any reason. Or for no reason at all.

And the treatment in those squalid cells was horrific.

She shivered at the memory.

"You're among friends now," Leo told her. "And Anna can meet you somewhere else if you prefer. I'm sure she would understand if we need to postpone the meeting."

"I'm fine," Rose managed.

He eyed her with concern, but when she didn't show him any sign of weakness he nodded and moved on. They walked on until they reached a door with a sensor, where Leo placed his hand against it and it slid open.

Inside, Anna sat on the far side of a large, gleaming white table with two raised rings protruding from its surface.

"Thank you so much for coming, Rose," Anna said with a welcoming smile that actually managed to set Rose at ease a little. "Please, have a seat."

She patted the chair next to her.

Rose walked over to sit beside her, thinking it was odd to sit beside the boss.

"See you later, ladies," Leo said, giving a wave. "I'm heading back to check on the engine room guys."

Anna blew him a kiss and he pretended to catch it before he headed out the door again.

"I have a proposal for you, Rose," Anna said. "I hope you'll keep an open mind about it."

"Of course," Rose told her.

"Juno let me know that it was unlikely you would agree to help, and I understand her reasoning," Anna said carefully. "But I see the way you look out for this ship and its interests. And I hope you will be willing to assist us in another matter."

Rose nodded.

"You've been an excellent addition to Agro, but your military training makes you eligible for a new position," Anna explained. "One that comes with a promotion to Lieutenant, and the commensurate pay raise, of course."

"That sounds amazing," Rose told her, desperately trying not to calculate how much of that pay raise could go home to Terra-4 to help the neighborhood. That was a full four pay levels over what she made now. "But keep in mind, my military experience was mostly in Agro. I did basic combat training, but primarily it was civilian-level work."

"That's why we would give you the promotion," Anna said. "This job is above civilian-level."

"What's the job?" Rose asked.

"There is a prisoner here in holding," Anna said. "And he doesn't belong here. I would like to have him remanded into your custody."

"What's he in for?" Rose asked, mystified.

Why would Anna think she was suited for this assignment? She didn't have any experience with guarding prisoners.

"His name is Rex Tylarr. He was our head of security until a few days ago, and he saved Ambassador Scott's life during the assassination attempt," Anna said, with feeling. "He's in here because he's a Cerulean."

Rage began to buzz in Rose's chest.

"Say something, Rose," Anna said.

"No thank you," Rose managed.

"That's all?" Anna replied.

"I'm not interested," Rose said, through clenched teeth.

"I don't want to pressure you, Rose," Anna said carefully. "But this is important. You'll just be holding him on house arrest with a proximity device. And it's only until we get to a port that has a trial by jury system."

"Look, I didn't come halfway around the universe just to babysit a Cerulean to save him from lock-up," Rose said, her temper getting the best of her as she'd been afraid it would. "They certainly don't mind locking up Terrans back home."

"Rose, he's a good man," Anna said softly.

"Oh, poor him, getting locked up and judged because of his race," Rose said. "That's what Ceruleans do to my people every day."

"He'll stay with you for a few days, and then it will be over," Anna said. "But you'll keep the pay raise for as long as you serve on my ship."

"There's not enough room in my quarters," Rose said automatically.

"We've already moved your things to a suite on the upper levels," Anna admitted.

"You assumed you could buy me?" Rose asked, feeling stung.

"I didn't want to pressure you with this," Anna said. "But Ambassador Scott asked for you personally."

Ambassador Scott.

She was the politician who was trying to end Cerulean occupation of Terran planets.

She was the person Rose had met, with stars in her eyes, grateful that someone in power wanted to help a Terran like her.

Rose had thanked Ambassador Scott, and offered to be at her service anytime, in any way that the ambassador wanted.

She hadn't expected anything like this.

Rose opened her mouth to speak, but then closed it again. What was she supposed to say?

A sensor beeped, jarring her out of her thoughts, and the door to the room slid open.

A huge Cerulean staggered in. He wore nothing but a pair of torn leather breeches. A black tattoo curled around one side of his massive blue chest.

His dark hair hung lank around his shoulders. His beard didn't cover the swelling and bruising on one side of his jaw. On the other side his eye was nearly swollen shut, and dried blood ran in rusty rivulets into the beard.

He looked up at her with his good eye.

A lightning flash of recognition went through Rose.

She had seen him before on the ship, before his imprisonment, at Juno's wedding. But it was his *expression* she recognized more than his face.

He was furious. As much as she was.

For an instant, she felt a burning kinship.

"Sit down, please," the guard behind him said quietly.

The big Cerulean looked away and the strange connection between them was broken, to Rose's relief.

"Rose, this is Rex," Anna said. "He was our head of security until recently. I think you may have seen him on duty at Princess Juno and Crown Prince Zane's wedding."

Rex looked pointedly down at his hands, which were now chained to the two rings in the table.

Fresh blood was beginning to seep from his injured eye.

"Did you not give him medical treatment before jailing him?" Rose heard herself ask.

"He wasn't injured in the attack," Anna said softly.

Rose studied his injuries again, taking it in.

"So these were inflicted while he was in custody?" she asked.

"He won't confirm it," Anna said, as if Rex weren't sitting right there. "But you can imagine that the others might view him as a traitor since he squelched their assassination attempt and saved Ambassador Scott."

"What the fuck are you doing back there?" Rose yelled at the guard as she jumped out of her chair before she knew what she was doing. "It's your job to safeguard those prisoners, not let them kill each other like animals."

The guard blinked at her with frightened eyes.

"No," Rex said, breaking his silence at last.

Everyone turned to him.

"This is a luxury cruiser, not a prison," Rex continued in a deep, calm voice. "The biggest job the security staff here should have is to deal with a guest who's had a few too many cocktails and might need to dry out for a night. We're not set up to hold a military coup as prisoners. Security is doing the best they can."

Rose blinked at him, opened her mouth, closed it again, and sat down, at a loss for words once more.

She she had to admit to herself that she had some

grudging respect for the Cerulean, even if she would never come out and say it to anyone else.

"Rose, if you agree to this, we will all be so grateful," Anna said softly. "Please, help us do the right thing."

In spite of her best efforts, Rose felt her resolve crack.

But she couldn't trust herself to say it out loud.

Instead, she gazed directly into Anna's eyes and nodded once in surrender.

Thank you, Lieutenant Mendez," Anna replied.

Thanks for reading the sample of **Conquered Mate!**

Want to see what happens when these two sworn enemies get a whole lot closer than either of them ever imagined?

Are you ready for for Rose and Rex to be forced to work together to solve a mystery full of stolen goods, intergalactic smugglers, a mysterious creature lurking in the forest, and more romantic tension than you can fit in a luxury space cruiser?

Then grab your copy of Conquered Mate: Stargazer Alien Space Cruise Brides #3!

https://www.tashablack.com/sascb.html

TASHA BLACK STARTER LIBRARY

Packed with steamy shifters, mischievous magic, billionaire superheroes, and plenty of HEAT, the Tasha Black Starter Library is the perfect way to dive into Tasha's unique brand of Romance with Bite!
Get your FREE books now at tashablack.com!

ABOUT THE AUTHOR

Tasha Black lives in a big old Victorian in a tiny college town. She loves reading anything she can get her hands on, writing paranormal romance, and sipping pumpkin spice lattes.

Get all the latest info, and claim your FREE Tasha Black Starter Library at www.TashaBlack.com

Plus you'll get the chance for sneak peeks of upcoming titles and other cool stuff!

Keep in touch...
www.tashablack.com
authortashablack@gmail.com

facebook.com/romancewithbite
twitter.com/romancewithbite

Made in United States
Troutdale, OR
07/07/2023

11036212R00096